Mary Stewart, one of the most popular novelists, was born in Sunderland, County Durham and lives in the West Highlands. Her first novel, *Madam, Will You Talk?* was published in 1955 and marked the beginning of a long and acclaimed writing career. All her novels have been bestsellers on both sides of the Atlantic. She was made a Doctor of Literature by Durham University in 2009.

Praise for Mary Stewart and *The Gabriel Hounds*:

'The world's leading romantic-suspense writer'
Sunday Times

'Probably the best Stewart yet' *Daily Mirror*

'She set the bench mark for pace, suspense and romance – with a great dollop of escapism as the icing' Elizabeth Buchan

'A comfortable chair and a Mary Stewart: total heaven. I'd rather read her than most other authors.' Harriet Evans

MARY STEWART

The Gabriel Hounds

HODDER

First published in Great Britain in 1967 by Hodder & Stoughton
An Hachette UK company

This edition 2011

1

A CIP catalogue record for this title is available from the British Library.

ISBN 978 1 444 72054 9

Printed and bound in the UK by
CPI Mackays, Chatham ME5 8TD

Hodder & Stoughton policy is to use papers that are natural, renewable and
recyclable products and made from wood grown in sustainable forests. The
logging and manufacturing processes are expected to conform to the
environmental regulations of the country of origin.

Hodder & Stoughton Ltd
338 Euston Road
London NW1 3BH

www.hodder.co.uk

For
Helen King

Author's Note

This story is freely based on the accounts of the life of the Lady Hester Stanhope. I have tried to shorten my references as much as possible, but for those who are interested, the list of books of page 92 wiil act as a guide and also an acknowledgement of my main sources. My debt to Doughty's *Travels in Arabia Deserta*, and also to Robin Fedden's marvellous *Syria and Lebanon* (John Murray) will be more than obvious.

One other word may perhaps be necessary. In a story of this sort it is inevitable that officials are mentioned by office, if not by name. Any references to Government bodies, Cabinet Ministers, frontier officials, etc., are made purely for the purposes of this story, and do not refer to any actual holders of these offices, living or dead. Moreover, though the Adonis Valley certainly exists, the Nahr el-Sal'q – with the village and the palace of Dar Ibrahim – does not.

I should also like to thank all those friends, from Edinburgh to Damascus, who have given me so much generous help.

M. S.

I

No vain discourse shalt thou hear therein:
Therein shall be a gushing fountain;
Therein shall be raised couches,
And goblets ready placed,
And cushions laid in order,
And carpets spread forth.

The Koran: Sura lxxxvii

I MET him in the street called Straight.

I had come out of the dark shop doorway into the dazzle of the Damascus sun, my arms full of silks. I didn't see anything at first, because the sun was right in my eyes and he was in shadow, just where the Straight Street becomes a dim tunnel under its high corrugated iron roof.

The souk was crowded. Someone stopped in front of me to take a photograph. A crowd of youths went by, eyeing me and calling comments in Arabic, punctuated by 'Miss' and 'Allo' and 'Goodbye'. A small grey donkey pattered past under a load of vegetables three times its own width. A taxi shaved me so near that I took a half step back into the shop doorway, and the shopkeeper, at my elbow, put out a protective hand for his rolls of silk. The taxi swerved, horn blaring, past the donkey, parted a tight group of ragged children the way a ship parts water, and aimed without any slackening of speed at the bottleneck where the street narrowed sharply between jutting rows of stalls.

It was then that I saw him. He had been standing, head bent, in front of a jeweller's stall, turning over some small gilt trinket in his hand. At the blast of the taxi's horn he glanced up, and stepped quickly out of the way. The step took him from black shadow full into the sun's glare, and, with a queer jerk of the heart, I saw who it was. I had known he was in this part of the world, and I suppose it was no odder to meet him in the middle of Damascus than anywhere else, but I stood there in the sunlight gazing, I suppose rather blankly, at the averted profile, four years strange to me, yet so immediately familiar, and somehow so inevitably here.

The taxi vanished into the black tunnel of the main souk with a jarring of gears and another yell of its horn. Between us the dirty hot street was empty. One of the rolls of silk slipped from my hands, and I grabbed for it, to catch it in a cascade of crimson just before it reached the filthy ground. The movement and the blinding colour must have caught his attention, for he turned, and our eyes met. I saw them widen, then he dropped the gilt object back on the jeweller's stall, and, ignoring the stream of bad American which the man was shouting after him, crossed the street towards me. The years rolled back more swiftly even than the crimson silk as he said, with exactly the same intonation with which a small boy had daily greeted his even smaller worshipper:

'Oh, hullo! It's you!'

I wasn't a small girl any more, I was twenty-two, and this was only my cousin Charles, whom of course I didn't worship any more. For some reason it seemed important to make this clear. I tried to echo his tone, but only managed to achieve a sort of idiotic deadpan calm. 'Hullo. How nice to see you. How you've grown!'

'Haven't I just, and I shave nearly every week now.' He grinned at me, and suddenly it wasn't the small boy any more. 'Christy love, thank goodness I've found you! What in the world are you doing here?'

'Didn't you know I was in Damascus?'

'I knew you were coming, but I couldn't find out when. I meant, what are you doing on your own? I thought you were here with a package tour?'

'Oh, I am,' I said, 'I just got kind of detached. Did Mummy tell you about it?'

'She told my mother, who passed it on to me, but nobody seemed very clear what you were doing or just when you'd be here, or even where you'd be staying. You might have known I'd want to catch up with you. Don't you ever give anyone your address?'

'I thought I had.'

'You did tell your mother a hotel, but it was the wrong one. When I rang them up they told me your group had gone to Jerusalem, and when I telephoned there they referred me back to Damascus. You cover your tracks well, young Christy.'

'I'm sorry,' I said, 'if I'd known there was a chance of

meeting you before Beirut . . . Our itinerary was changed, that's all, something to do with the flight bookings, so we're doing the tour back to front, and they had to alter the Damascus hotel. Oh, blast, and we leave for Beirut tomorrow! We've been here three days now. Have you been here all the time?'

'Only since yesterday. The man I have to see in Damascus isn't coming home till Saturday, but when I was told you'd be about due to arrive here, I came straight up. As you say, blast. Look, perhaps it's a good thing they've turned your tour arsy-versy – you needn't go tomorrow, surely? I've got to wait here till the weekend myself, so why don't you cut loose from your group and we'll do Damascus together and then go on to Beirut? You're not bound to stay with them, are you?' He looked down at me, raising his brows. 'What on earth are you doing in a package tour, anyway? I wouldn't have thought it was exactly your thing?'

'I suppose not, but I got a sudden yen to see this part of the world, and I didn't know a thing about it, and they make it so easy – they do everything about bookings and things, and there's a courier who speaks Arabic and knows the score. I couldn't very well come on my own, could I?'

'I don't see why not. And don't look at me with those great big helpless eyes, either. If any female was ever entirely capable of looking after herself, it's you.'

'Oh, sure, Black Belt of the nth degree, that's me.' I regarded him with pleasure. 'Oh, Charles, believe it or not, it's marvellous to see you! Thank goodness your mother caught up with you and told you I'd be here! It'd have been lovely to have some time here with you, but it can't be helped. I'd planned to wait around in Beirut after the rest of my group goes home on Saturday, so I'll stick to that, I think. Have you had a good trip? A sort of Grand Tour, wasn't it, with Robbie?'

'Sort of. Seeing the world and brushing up my Arabic before doing some real work in Beirut. Oh, it all went like a bomb ... We drove down through France and shipped the car to Tangier and then ambled along through North Africa. Robbie had to go home from Cairo, so I came on alone. It was in Cario that I got Mother's letter saying you were coming on this trip of yours, so I came straight up, hoping we'd coincide.'

'Did you say you had to see someone here? Business?'

'Partly. Look, what are we standing here for? This place smells, and any minute now we'll be mown down by one of these donkeys. Come and have some tea.'

'Love to, but where do you propose to find tea in the middle of Damascus?'

'In my little pad, which is the nearest thing to the Azem Palace you ever saw.' He grinned. 'I'm not at an hotel, I'm staying with a man I knew at Oxford, Ben Sifara, I don't know whether you ever heard your father mention the name? Ben's father's a bit of a VIP in Damascus – knows everyone and owns a bit of everything, has a brother banking in Beirut and a brother-in-law in the Cabinet – Minister of the Interior, no less. The family's what they call a "good family" over here, which in Syria just means stinking rich.'

'Nice going. At that rate we'd be well up in the stud book.'

'Well, aren't we?' My cousin was crisply ironic. I knew what he meant. My own family of merchant bankers had been stinking rich for three generations, and it was surprising how many people were willing to overlook the very mixed, not to say plain bastard blood that pumped through the Mansel veins.

I laughed. 'I suppose he's a business contact of Daddy and Uncle Chas?'

'Yes. Ben made me promise to look him up if ever I was in Syria, and Father was keen for me to make contact, so here I am.'

'Big deal. Well, I'd love to come. Just wait a moment till I get my silk.' I considered the brilliant mass in my arms. 'The only thing is, which?'

'I'm not wild keen on either, if you want the truth.' My cousin lifted a fold, felt it, frowned on it, and let it fall. 'Nice texture, but the red's rather fierce, isn't it? People'd post letters in you. And the blue. . . ? not, but not, for you, my love. It doesn't suit me, and I like my girls to tone.'

I regarded him coldly. 'And just for that I'll buy them both and have them made up in stripes. Horizontal. No, I do rather see what you mean. They looked all right in the shop.'

'Since they keep it pitch dark in there, they would.'

'Well, fair enough, I wanted it for a dressing-gown. Perhaps in a dim light . . . ? I mean, the pattern's rather nice and Eastern . . . ?'

'No.'

'The sickening thing about you,' I said bitterly, 'is that you're sometimes right. What were you buying for yourself along Woolworth Alley, if it comes to that? A ring for Emily?'

'A jewel for my love, certainly. A blue bead for my car.'

'A blue bead for your—? A *blue bead* for your car? Now this I really do not believe!'

He laughed. 'Don't you know? Blue beads ward off the Evil Eye. All the camels and donkeys wear them, so why not the car? They sometimes have rather fetching turquoise ones. Never mind now, I can get one any time. Do you really want some silk? Have a heart, anything you get at home will be just as good, and you won't have the trouble of carrying it.'

The shopkeeper, who was just behind me, and whose presence we had both completely forgotten, here said with justifiable bitterness: 'We do all right till you come, The lady had very good taste.'

'I'm sure she had,' said my cousin, 'but you can't expect me to stand for a dressing-gown in pillar-box red or budgie blue. If you've anything else more suitable perhaps you'll show it to us.'

The man's expression lightened to pleased comprehension, and, as he took in my cousin's obviously expensive clothes, anticipation. 'I understand. Forgive, sir. You are the lady's husband.'

'Not yet,' said Charles. 'Come on, Christy, let's go in and buy it, and then get out of this and go where we can talk. My car's in the square at the end of the street. Where is your party, by the way?'

'I don't know, I lost them. We'd been through the Great Mosque, and then we were all trailing in a sort of croc through the souks and I stopped to look at the stalls, and then they'd sort of gone.'

'And you let them go? Won't they start combing the souks with bloodhounds when they find you're missing?'

'Probably.' I gathered up the silks and turned to the shop doorway. 'Charles, if there was some really luscious off-white—'

'Seriously, hadn't you better telephone the hotel?'

I shrugged. 'I doubt if they'll even miss me before dinner. They're used to me wandering off by now.'

'Still the same spoiled little madam I love?'

'I just don't like crowds. Anyway, look, who's talking! Daddy always said you were spoiled rotten yourself, and it's true, so help me.'

'But yes. Dear Uncle Chris,' said my cousin placidly, following me into the black cave of the shop.

In the end I did buy white, some lovely heavy off-white brocade which, not much to my surprise, Charles seemed to conjure from some dim shelf which the shopkeeper hadn't previously shown me. Moreover, it was cheaper than anything I had yet seen. Nor did it come as much of a surprise to hear Charles talking to the shopkeeper and his assistant in slowish but what seemed to be passably fluent Arabic. He might (as my parents had often told one another in my hearing) be 'spoiled rotten', but nobody had ever denied that he had considerable intelligence when he chose to use it – which was (as they insisted) about once a month, and then entirely in his own interests.

When we had reached the square, followed by the shop boy carrying the silk, Charles's car was instantly recognizable – not by its make or colour, neither of which could be seen, but by the six-deep crowd of small boys who stood round it. On investigation it proved to be a white Porsche 911 S. And because I loved my cousin and knew my stuff, I promptly gave him his cue.

'What a little beauty! How do you like her?'

He told me. He opened the bonnet and showed me. He almost stripped her down to demonstrate to me. The small boys loved it. They crowded in, twelve deep now, open-mouthed and staring, and probably taking in rather more than I did of the MacPherson struts and lower wishbones, compression ratios and torques and telescopic dampers . . . I let the loverlike phrases roll over me and watched my cousin's face and hands and remembered all the other times – the electric train set, the kestrel's egg, the first wristwatch, the bicycle . . .

He straightened up, hauled a couple of boys backwards out of the engine and shut the bonnet, paid off the two biggest who had presumably been on guard for him, and gave the shop boy a tip that startled him into fervent speech. We drove off.

'What's he saying?'

'Just "thank you". In other words, "The blessing of Allah be upon you, your children, and your children's children."' The car threaded its competent way out of the packed square, and turned down a narrow rutted street with every telescopic damper working overtime. 'This means you, more or less. I hope we're still engaged?'

'*Faute de mieux*, I suppose we are. But I seem to remember that you broke it off yourself, and in writing, when you met that blonde female – what was her name, the model? The one that looked like a Belsen case.'

'Samantha? She was very chic.'

'Oh, sure. They have to look that anyway, don't they, so that they can wear all that far-out clobber standing up to their knees in the sea, or stable straw, or empty Coke bottles or something. What happened to Samantha?'

'Probably met her just fate, but not with me.'

'Well, that was ages ago – just after the last time we met. No one else in my way? You can't tell me you've been going straight for four years?'

'Are you joking?' He changed down, turned sharp left and accelerated down another filthy little alley with a total width of about a yard and a half. 'But actually, yes. Virtually, if you get me.'

'I get you. What happened to Emily?'

'Who the devil's Emily?'

'Wasn't it Emily? Last year, I'm sure Mummy said Emily – or was it Myrtle? The names you pick.'

'I can't see that any of them are worse than Christabel.'

I laughed. 'You have a point there.'

'As far as I'm concerned,' said my cousin, 'we're still pledged as from the cradle. The lovely lolly is still in the

family, and Great-Grandfather Rosenbaum, on whom
be peace, can stop whirling in his whited sepulchre as
from now, so—'

'Mind that puppy!'

'It's all right, I saw it – at least, the Porsche did. So
that's settled. *Also gut!*'

'You take a lot for granted, don't you? Just because I
stayed faithful all my teens, even when you had spots.'

'A fat lot of chance you had to be anything else,' said
my cousin. 'You were as fat as a seal puppy yourself. I
must say you've improved.' A sideways look, summa-
rily brotherly, with rather less sexual appraisement
than a dog-show judge. 'In fact you're rather gorgeous,
coz, and I like that dress. Well, blight my hopes if you
must. Is there someone?'

I grinned. 'Watch it, love, or you'll find it's for real,
and you'll be selling your car to buy a diamond.'

'Suits me,' he said lightly. 'And here we are.'

The Porsche slowed down and turned at right angles
out of the street into a small unappetising courtyard,
where the sun struck blindly down into the dust, and
two cats slept on a stack of battered petrol cans. In one
corner was a wedge of indigo shade, and into this, with
an elegant economy of effort, he drove the car and
parked it.

'Front entrance. Damascus style, Looks like nothing
on earth, doesn't it? Come in.'

It didn't look at first as if the courtyard could be the
entrance to anything. It was boxed, stiflingly, by its
high, blind walls, and smelt of hens and stale urine. But
at one side a big archway was forbiddingly blocked by a

door whose warped timbers still held, in the massive wrought handle and hinges, a hint of some ancient splendour. Charles opened the door on a black passageway, which gave at the other end on an arch of light. We went through.

The light came from a second courtyard, this time an oblong about the size of a tennis court, with pointed Moorish arches on three sides holding a shady cloister, and on the fourth, at the end of the court, a raised platform or dais behind a triple arch, which made a kind of stage or small inner room. The back and sides of this dais were furnished with wide bench seats set against the wall, and I recognized the 'divan' or place where men of the East meet and talk. Even in modern Eastern houses today the sitting-rooms are often arranged like this, traditionally, with chairs and sofas backed against the wall on three sides of the room. Low tables stood in front of the couches. In the middle of the court a fountain played; the floor was tiled with blue and white, and the miniature colonnade was jewelled and glittering with mosaics in blue and green and gilt. A turtle dove crooned somewhere, orange trees stood here and there in tubs, and where the fountain splashed I caught the gleam of gold fin. The court was very cool, and smelt of orange-blossom.

'Come into the divan,' said Charles. 'Yes, it's rather lovely, isn't it? There's something very satisfying about Arab building, I always think – all poetry and passion and romance, but very elegant with it. Like their literature, if it comes to that. But you ought to see the furniture; my bedroom's done up with the rejects from Bluebeard's chamber.'

'I know what you mean, I saw some choice pieces in those homey little rooms in the Azem Palace – all inlaid with mother-of-pearl like smallpox, or else pure Victorian and made of arthritic bamboos. But oh, Charles, the rugs! Look at those . . . and that blue one on the couch . . . am I really allowed to sit on it?'

'Go right ahead. I think Ben'll be in soon, but meanwhile, as he keeps telling me, his house is mine, so what would you like? Tea?'

'I think I'd rather have coffee. What do you do, clap your hands and summon the eunuchs?'

'More or less.' There was a little brass bell on the quite hideous inlaid table in front of me. He picked this up and rang it, then prowled restlessly – he had always been restless – down the steps of the divan as far as the fountain, waiting. I sat down on the beautiful blue rug, leaned against the cushions, and watched him.

No, he hadn't changed. As children, we were always supposed to be very much alike, Charles and I; in fact, when we were small, people had taken us for twins. This had always infuriated Charles, who in those days had been aggressively masculine, but to me, dumbly worshipping my clever cousin as only a small girl can, it had been a delight. As we grew up the resemblance had, of course, faded. There were still the basic similarities, the dark hair, high Slav cheekbones, slightly aquiline nose, grey eyes and spare build. Now he was some inches taller than I, and he had broadened, but had seemingly reacted from the aggressive masculinity of adolescence towards a sort of carefully casual elegance which somehow suited him, and oddly enough was no less male. He had on his North African travels acquired a fine tan, and this made his eyes look lighter than my own, though this may only have been in contrast to the black lashes which were (in Nature's unfair way) longer and thicker than mine. Be that as it may, Charles's eyes were beautiful, dark grey and thickly fringed. Occasionally still, I thought, the resemblance between us must be striking; a turn of the head, a trick of the voice, a movement. What we certainly had in common was the 'spoiled' quality that we were so quick to recognise in one another; a flippant cleverness that could become waspish, an arrogance that did not spring from any pride of achievement but was, I am afraid, the result of having too much too young; a fiercely self-conscious rejecting of any personal ties (including those of our families) which we called independence, but which was really an almost morbid fear of possessiveness; and something we called sensitivity, which probably only meant that our skins were too thin for our own comfort.

Perhaps I should explain here that the relationship between Charles and myself was rather closer than that between ordinary cousins. Our fathers, Charles and Christopher Mansel, were identical twins who had been, almost up to the time they were married, both inseparable and indistinguishable, and they had in fact married on the same day – girls who bore no relation to one another, but who (as one could see still) had been of much the same physical type. And happily the two

Mrs Mansels liked one another immensely – happily, because Charles and Christopher were business part- ners, and when the elder twin had inherited the family house in Kent, the younger, Christopher, had built one for himself within a mile of it. So Charles's son and Christopher's daughter had been brought up together until four years ago, when Christopher had exported his family – Mummy and myself – to Los Angeles, from which earthly paradise we had escaped occasion- ally to stay at Charles's home, ours being let for the duration. But my visits there had never coincided with my cousin's. In the intervals of Oxford he had spent his time abroad, enjoying himself doing what he called 'looking around', and indulging the flair for languages which was part of our heritage from a mongrel ances- try, and which young Charles intended to turn to account when he went into one of the family's Con- tinental banks. I had not flown so high. I had brought nothing home from Los Angeles except an American flair for dressing, an accent which I lost as soon as I reasonably could, and three years' experience of the frenetic world of American commercial television, where I had served a wild apprenticeship as producer's assistant in a small company calling itself Sunshine Television Incorporated – this apparently in blissful ignorance of the fact that like most companies it was normally referred to by its initials, *S.T. Inc.*

Now here we were again, my cousin and I, and back without effort on the same terms. It was not that we had been, like our fathers, inseparable – that wasn't possible. What had held us so easily together was, paradoxically enough, a sort of mutual rejection. We had each recognised in the other a refusal to be claimed, and respected this. This had made tolerable – and even funny – the thin-worn family joke about our engagement, and all the cooings over us and 'how lovely it would be . . .' that we had had to endure as children. The cradle-made match of the joke had not in fact come from our parents – I had heard my father insisting that the family characteristics were bad enough singly, but squared they would undoubtedly produce criminal lunatics, where upon Charles's father would retort that nothing could be more likely in a match that was practically incest, but that since my mother was partly Irish, and Charles's half-Austrian, half-Russian with French overtones (as her husband put it) the stock might be strong enough to stand it. We also had a Polish Jew, a Dane and a German among our assorted great-grandparents, and counted ourselves English, which was fair enough.

But the auntly cooings over the two charming children (as I believe we were) had gone on, and Charles and I had listened, fought, hated and defended one another, and stayed together. It had occurred to neither of us in actual fact that we could be the object of one another's sexual stirrings – it would, at sixteen or seventeen, have indeed been incest. So, as much proof against one another as brother and sister, we had watched with equal amusement and derision each other's first romantic adventures.

The affairs were brief, and inevitable. Sooner or later the girl would start assuming a claim on Charles, and be dropped without trace. Or, somehow, my own pin-up would lose his gloss, Charles would say something less than forgiveable about him, I would retort furiously, then laugh and agree, and life would be whole once more.

And our respective parents bore with us lovingly through it all, took off the leading strings, gave us the money, listened to what mattered and forgot the rest, possibly because they wanted freedom from us as urgently as we thought we wanted freedom from them. The result was that we went back to them at intervals like homing bees, and we were happy. Perhaps they saw more clearly than could Charles and I, the basic security in our lives which made his restlessness and my indecisiveness nothing more than the taking of soundings outside the harbour. Perhaps they could even see, through it all, the end that would come.

But here we were at the beginning. A young Arab in white had brought in a tray holding an elaborately chased copper urn and two small blue cups which he set on the table in front of me. He said something to Charles, and went out. My cousin came quickly up the steps of the divan and sat down beside me.

'He says Ben won't be in just yet, not until evening. Go on, you pour.'

'Is his mother away, too?'

'His mother's dead. His father's sister runs the place for them, but she lives retired, as they say. No, *not* a harem, so don't look so curious and hopeful; she merely has a long siesta and won't come out till dinner-time. Smoke?'

'Not now. I don't much, as a matter of fact, only now and again for effect, rather silly. Good heavens, what are those? Hashish or something?'

'No, absolutely harmless. Egyptian. They do look awful, don't they? Well now, tell me what you've been doing.'

He accepted the cup of strong black coffee from me and curled back on the silk-covered seat, waiting expectantly.

Four years of gossip is a lot to catch up on, and we had never been letter-writers. I suppose more than an hour had gone by, and the sun had moved over to leave half the court in shadow before my cousin stretched, stubbed out another Egyptian cigarette and said: 'Look, what's all this about sticking with your group? Won't you change your mind and cut loose now? Stay till Sunday, and I'll drive you up – the Barada Valley's lovely and there's a good road.'

'Thanks all the same, but I'd better stay with them. We're doing that run by car in any case, and having a look at Baalbek on the way.'

'I'd take you there.'

'It would be smashing, but it's all fixed, and as a matter of fact I've packed, and you know there's all that silly business with visas here. Mine's dated tomorrow, and there's this business of a group passport, and there was such a hooha anyway about my staying behind after the group leaves for England on Saturday that I can't face it all over again. I think I'll just go.'

'All right, then, I'll see you in Beirut. Where are you staying?'

'I thought I'd move to the Phoenicia once I'm on my own.'

'I'll join you there. Book in for me, will you? I'll telephone you before I leave Damascus. What had you planned to do with the extra time, apart – I suppose – from going up to Dar Ibrahim?'

'Dar Ibrahim?' I repeated blankly.

'Great-Aunt Harriet's place. That's its name, surely you knew? It's on the Nahr Ibrahim, the Adonis river.'

'I – yes, I suppose I knew, but I'd forgotten. Goodness, Great-Aunt Harriet . . . I never thought . . . Is it near Beirut, then?'

'About thirty miles away, along the coast road to Byblos and then inland into the mountains, up towards the source of the Adonis. The road runs up the ridge on the north side of the valley, and somewhere between Tourzaya and Qartaba there's a tributary river called the Nahr el-Sal'q that goes tumbling down to meet the Adonis. Dar Ibrahim's in the middle of the valley, where the rivers meet.'

'Have you ever been there?'

'No, but I'm planning to. D'you really mean you hadn't thought about it?'

'Not a flicker of a thought. I'd certainly intended to go up the Adonis Valley and see the source where the cascade is, and the temple of Whoever-it-is, and the place where Venus and Adonis met – in fact I was thinking of hiring a car for the trip on Sunday, after the group go . . . But to be honest I'd forgotten all about Aunt H. I hardly even remember her, you know, we were in Los Angeles when she was home last, and before that it was – heavens, it must be all of fifteen years! And Mummy never said a thing about this place of hers – Dar Ibrahim, was that the name? – but that's probably only because her geography's about on par with mine and she'd never realised Beirut was so near.' I put down my cup. 'Right in the Adonis Valley? Well, I might go with you, at that, if only to see the place and tell Daddy what it was like. I'm sure he'd think there was hope for me yet if I told him I'd trekked up there to put some flowers on the old dear's grave.'

'She'd probably kick you in the teeth if you tried,' said Charles. 'She's very much alive. You really are a teeny bit out of touch, aren't you?'

I stared. 'Alive? Aunt H? Now who's out of touch? She died just after the New Year.'

He laughed. 'Not she. If you're thinking about the Last Will and Testament, that's nothing to go by, in the last few years she's sent them round about once every six months. Didn't Uncle Chris get the famous letter renouncing her British nationality and finally cutting everyone off with sixpence? Everyone except me, that is.' He grinned. 'And I was to have the Gabriel Hounds and her copy of the Koran because I showed signs of taking a "reasonable interest in the real civilisations of the world". That was because I was learning Arabic. In some ways,' added my cousin thoughtfully, 'she must still be very innocent if she thinks Mansel and Mansel takes an interest in anything whatever except for the basest of all possible reasons.'

'Look, come off it, you're kidding me.'

'About the Wills and so on? Indeed I'm not. She

renounced us in beautiful round early-Victorian terms
– her letters were period pieces, you know – the family,
Britain, God, the lot. Well, perhaps not God exactly,
but she was going to turn Mohammedan, and would
we please send out a reliable English stonemason to
build a private cemetery where she could rest for ever
in the peace of Allah among her beloved dogs, and
would we also inform the Editor of *The Times* that the
paper of the overseas edition was too thin to allow her
to do the crossword puzzles properly, and she would
like it changed.'

'You can't be serious.'

'As an owl,' said my cousin. 'I swear to every word.'

'And what in the world are the Gabriel Hounds?'

'Don't you remember them? I suppose you don't.'

'I seem to remember the phrase, that's all. Wasn't it
something in a story?'

'A legend in that book we had called "North-Country
Tales", or some such title. The Gabriel Hounds are
supposed to be a pack of hounds that run with
death, and when someone's going to die you hear them
howling over the house at night. I think myself that the
idea must have come from the wild geese – have you
heard them? They sound like a pack of hounds in full
cry overhead, and the old name for them used to be
"gabble ratchet". I've sometimes wondered if the "Gabriel" doesn't come from "gabble", because after all
Gabriel wasn't the angel of death . . .' He glanced
across. 'You shivered. Are you cold?'

'No. One of them gabbling over my grave, I expect.
What have they to do with Great-Aunt Harriet?'

'Nothing, really, except that she had a pair of china dogs I lusted after, and I christened them the Gabriel Hounds because they were like the illustrations in the book.'

'A pair of – oh, no, really, you must be out of your tiny mind. That's schizophrenia, or is it skitso? Nobody in this world can want to own a white Porsche with one hand and a pair of china dogs with the other! I don't believe it.'

He laughed. 'Real china, Christy love, Chinese china . . . They're Ming as ever was, and probably museum pieces. Heaven knows what they're worth now, but since I had the good taste to fall flat in love with them at the age of six, and Great-Aunt Harriet with even better taste fell flat in love with me at the same time, she promised them to me. And stark raving bonkers though she undoubtedly is now, she seems to have remembered.' He made a restless movement. 'Oh, don't you see, it doesn't really matter about the dogs, they make a good excuse, that's all.'

'For going to see her?'

'Yes.'

'Family feeling cropping up a bit late in the day?' I said it derisively, but he didn't laugh or disclaim, as I had expected. He gave me an odd, slanting look from under the long lashes, and said merely: 'I don't want to pass up the chance. It sounds such a damned intriguing set-up.'

'Well, of course I'll go with you, out of sheer roaring curiosity, and let's hope she does remember you, because I'm darned sure she won't remember me. She must be at least a hundred.'

'Not a day over eighty, I swear, and active with it by all accounts. She's a local legend, goes galloping about the country-side on horseback with a gaggle of hounds and shoots whatever there is to shoot for her own dinner.'

'Gabble, you mean. I remember that about her, who could forget? When she stayed with us that time she brought eight King Charles spaniels.'

'It's Tibetan terriers now, and salukis – Persian greyhounds, the dogs the Arab princes used for hunting. Oh, she's gone the limit, I gather – turned Arab herself, male at that, dresses like an Emir, smokes a hubble-bubble, never sees anybody except at night, and lives in this dirty great palace—'

'Palace?' I said, startled. 'Who does she think she is? Lady Hester Stanhope?'

'Exactly that. Models herself on the story, one gathers. Even calls herself Lady Harriet, and as you and I well know, we've had a lot of queer things in the family, but never a Lady.' He stared, not flatteringly. 'What do you know about Lady Hester Stanhope?'

'Didn't I tell you? When we spent last Christmas at your house they put me in your room, and I read some of your books. You've an awful lot about the Middle East. Have you really read all that Arabian poetry and stuff? And the Koran?'

'All through.'

'Well, you might say it was your library that gave me the idea of seeing this part of the world in the first place. We always did go for the same things, didn't we – or maybe you'd say I tagged along where you went . . . ? I'd always had vaguely romantic ideas about Petra and Damascus and Palmyra, but never thought about really coming here; then I saw the advert for this package tour, so I thought I'd join up, find my way about, then stay on after they'd gone and take my time filling in a few extras. One of them was Djoun, Lady Hester Stanhope's place.'

'It's a ruin.'

'I know, but I still thought I'd like to see it. She was quite a girl, wasn't she? I read everything you had about her, and nice snappy reading it was, compared with some of those tomes of yours. I had flu just after Christmas and was stuck indoors for a fortnight, and Mummy hadn't time to rake round the bookshops for something more my weight.'

He grinned, undeceived. 'Don't work so hard at not being clever. I'm not one of your muscle-bound blonds.'

'Neither you are,' I said.

Our eyes met. There was a tiny silence, in which the fountain sounded oddly loud. Then my cousin got up and reached a hand. 'Come and see the water lilies now the sun's gone. They shut while you watch.'

I followed him down into the now coolly shadowed court. The lilies were pale blue, held on stiff stems a few inches above the water, where their glossy leaves overlapped the still surface like tiles of jade. Gold fins winked here and there below them, and a gold bee sipped water at a leaf's edge. A powder-blue petal shut, and another, till one by one the lilies were turbaned up, stiff and quiet for the night. Another late bee, almost caught by a folding flower, wrestled his way angrily out of the petals, and shot off like a bullet.

I watched half absently, my mind still busy with the recent fragments of information Charles had flung at me, the intriguing picture of the eccentric old lady who had dropped so long ago out of family reality into family legend. The picture Charles had just given me of her blurred and blended in the imagination with the vivid mental pictures I had built up during that Christmas period of enforced reading. It was true that I had found some of Charles's books heavy going, but the accounts of the eccentric Lady Hester had been extremely readable, not to say racy.

She had gone out to the Middle East in the early eighteen hundreds, an Earl's daughter in the days when rank counted for almost everything, a masculine peremptory woman who, as Pitt's niece, was also accustomed to political consequence. After travelling round in considerable state with a retinue which included lover, slaves, and attendant physician, she had decided to settle in Syria (as it then was) and eventually purchased for herself a mountain-top fortress near Djoun, not far from Sidon. There she had lived in Eastern state, dressing as a Turkish Emir, and ruling her household of servants, Albanian guards, Negro slaves, companions, grooms and personal doctor with a rod of iron and at times, literally, a whip. Her fortress, perched on a hot bare hilltop, was described by a contemporary as 'an enchanted palace', and was a world in itself of courtyards, corridors as complex as a Chinese puzzle, walled gardens approached by winding stairs, secret exits cut in the rock where the Lady's spies came and went, the whole exotic with murmuring fountains and luxuriant gardens. It was a deliberate re-creation of an Arabian Nights' wonderland with all the fantastic properties of Eastern fairytale solidly at hand. Roses and jasmine, mute black slaves and nightingales, camels and sacred cats and Arab horses, she had them all. Fearless, utterly selfish, arrogant and eccentric, and growing with the years beyond eccentricity into megalomania, she meddled in local politics, defied the local Emirs, and placed herself – with some success – above the law. She finally seems to have believed in her own mystical destiny as Queen of the East who would one day ride crowned into Jerusalem at the side of the new Messiah.

The end came as it comes to the determined *puissante et solitaire* – she died alone, old and destitute, her fortune spent, her fortress rotting around her, her servants robbing and neglecting her. But she left – along with her debts – a legend that persists to this day.

It was certainly intriguing to think that it might be persisting in one form in the person of my own Great-Aunt Harriet. From what I knew of the lady, I thought she would (apart from the rank) fit into the role quite well. She had wealth, considerable personality and some scholarship, and had travelled widely and with a retinue which, though not quite as impressive as Lady Hester Stanhope's in 1820, had created quite as much stir and trouble a hundred years later. She had married an archaeologist, Ernest Boyd, and thereafter accompanied him on all his working journeys, hanging over and (it must be confessed) superintending his 'digs' from Cambodia to the Euphrates Valley. After his death she gave up active work and returned to England, but continued to take deep interest in the Middle East, and financed one or two expeditions that stirred her fancy. Two years of England's weather had been enough. She had said goodbye to the family (this was the last visit that I remembered) and gone off to the Lebanon, where she had bought her hilltop refuge and settled down (she told us) to write a book.

From this fastness she had made one sortie, four years ago, just after my side of the family had gone to Los Angeles. She had come, she said, to settle her affairs – which meant removing her considerable assets to the Lebanon – pick up a mate for her revolting (Charles said) Tibetan terrier Delilah, and shake the mud of England off her skirts for good. This was the last I had heard. Whether she had in fact written anything at all during her fifteen years' exile nobody had any idea, except for the occasional re-makes of her Will, which the family read with pleasure and then disregarded. We could get along as well without Great-Aunt Harriet as it appeared she could without us. There was of course no resentment on either side; my great-aunt merely personified in herself the family's genius for detachment.

So I still regarded my cousin doubtfully. 'You think she'll see you?'

'Oh, she'll see me,' he said calmly. 'My mother was always pretty sarcastic about Great-Aunt Harriet's penchant for young men, but I see no reason why we shouldn't trade on it. And if I tell her I've come to demand my rights, viz. the Gabriel Hounds, it'll appeal to her; she was always a tough egg who liked people who stuck out for their dues. If I can get to Beirut by Sunday evening, what do you say we make a date of it together for Monday?'

'I'm on. It sounds intriguing, if I thought one could believe a word of it.'

'Sober truth – or as near sober truth as you'll ever get in this country,' promised my cousin. 'Don't you know what they say about it? That it's a country where anything can happen, a "country of prodigies . . ."' He quoted softly: ' "The men inhabiting this country of prodigies – those men of rocks and deserts – whose imagination is higher coloured and yet more cloudy than the horizon of their sands and their seas, act according to the word of Mahomet and Lady Hester Stanhope. They require commerce with the stars, with prophecies, miracles and the second sight of genius." '

'What's that?'

'Lamartine.'

'Makes it sound as if even Great-Aunt Harriet might be normal. I can hardly wait. But I'll have to go now.' I glanced at my watch. 'Heavens, yes, it's dinner-time.'

'I'm sure Ben would want you to stay. He'll be in any minute. Can't you?'

'I'd like to, but we've an early start tomorrow, and I've things to do.' I stooped to retrieve my handbag. 'And you're going to drive me home, dear boy, and no mistake. I'm not venturing through the dark streets of Damascus for you or anybody – even if I could find the way which I probably can't. Unless you simply lend me the Porsche?'

'There are some risks I will take,' said my cousin, 'and some I won't. I'll drive you back. Come along.'

We crossed the court quietly together. Someone – the Arab boy, probably – must have brought a lamp in and set it in a niche near the door. It was an Aladdin lamp of some silvery metal which was probably in daylight hideous; but in the dusk, and holding the small orange buds of flame, it looked quite beautiful. The deep blue oblong of sky above the open court was pricking already with brilliant stars. No ugly diffusion of city lights spoiled the deep velvet of that sky; even hanging as it was above the glittering and crowded richness of the Damascus oasis, it spoke of the desert and the vast empty silences beyond the last palm tree. The courtyard itself was quiet. The far murmur of city traffic, no louder than the humming in a shell, made a background to this still quiet, where the only sound was the trickle of the fountain. The well in the desert . . . A fish moved below the surface, and the flick of gold, caught by the lamp, seemed to underscore the beauty of the living water. One could almost hear the fish moving. A bird settled itself crooningly to sleep above the arcade in a rustle of leaves.

'A turtle dove, do you hear it?' Charles's voice, quiet as it was, made me jump. 'The poets say she calls all the time for her lover – "*Yusuf, Yusuf*", till her voice breaks in a sob. I'll ring you Saturday evening then, at the Phoenicia, to tell you when I'm coming.'

'I'll be waiting. I only hope that after all this we get

our Arabian Nights' Entertainment at Dar Ibrahim. Oh, *you* probably will, fascinating creature that you are, but is there the faintest reason why she should want to see me?'

'She'll be delighted to see you,' said my cousin generously. 'Damn it, I was even quite pleased to see you myself.'

'You must be slipping, paying me compliments like that,' I said, preceding him to the doorway.

2

Adonis
Who lives away in Lebanon,
In stony Lebanon, where blooms
His red anemone.

James Elroy Flecker: *Santorin*

I SUPPOSE I had assumed Charles to be exaggerating the Dar Ibrahim 'legend', but it seemed he was right. I found it quite easy to get news of my eccentric relative in Beirut, In fact, even had I never heard of her, she would have been brought to my notice.

It happened on Saturday, the day the group left for London, and I moved myself to the Phoenicia Hotel to plan my brief independence and wait for Charles. On what was left of the Saturday I wanted to get my hair done and do some shopping; then on Sunday I planned to hire a car and driver to take me exploring up into the Lebanon range to the source of the Adonis River.

It was when I approached the desk clerk in the hotel, to ask him to lay on a chauffeur-driven car for this trip, that I came across my great-aunt.

The clerk entered into my plans with enthusiasm,

almost managing to conceal his private thoughts about the inexplicable whims of tourists. If a young woman was eager to incur the expense of a car and driver to go up and look at a few dirty villages and a waterfall, then of course he would help her . . . and (I could see the expert assessment of my clothes, my room number, and my probable bill) the more expensive the car the better.

'And I understand,' I added, 'that right up at the Adonis Source there's the ruins of an old Roman temple, and another smaller one not too far away, that I might visit.'

'Yes?' said the clerk, then hurriedly changing his intonation: 'Yes, of course, temples.' He wrote something, passing the buck with some relief. 'I will tell the driver to include them in the itinerary.'

'Please do. What do we do about lunch?'

Now this, it seemed, was talking. He brightened immediately. There was the famous summer hotel – I had heard of it, no doubt? – where I could get an excellent meal, and with music. Oh, yes, there was music in every room, continuous music, taped round the clock, in case the mountain silence got you down. And a swimming-pool. And tennis. 'And then, of course, if you make a slight detour on your way back you'll be able to see Dar Ibrahim.'

He misunderstood the surprise on my face, and explained quickly: 'You have not heard of this? Oh, Dar Ibrahim's a palace where an English lady lives, a very old lady who used to be famous, and she bought this palace when it was falling into ruin and filled it with beautiful things and planted the gardens again, and in the old days famous people would go up to stay with her, and it was possible to see over some parts of the palace, just as today you can see Beit ed-Din and the Crusader Castles. But now, alas . . . she is old now, and they say a little—' he made an eloquent face and touched his forehead. 'The place is shut up now, and she sees no one, and she never leaves the palace. But I have heard what a wonderful place it used to be, and I have myself seen her riding out with her servants . . . but that is all changed, she is old, and it is a long time since anyone has seen her.'

'How long?'

He spread his hands. 'Six months, a year, I cannot say.'

'But she's still there?'

'Certainly. I believe I heard talk of a companion, but this may only be rumour. I think there are still two or three servants with her, and once a month supplies are sent from Beirut up to Sal'q – that's the nearest village, and taken across by mule.'

'Isn't there a road?'

'No. The road goes along the ridge above the valley, and to get to Dar Ibrahim from the village one must walk, or go by mule.' He smiled. 'I wasn't suggesting you should do this, because of course it's not worth it now, you can't get in. I was only recommending the view. It's very fine. In any case, Dar Ibrahim looks all the better from a distance.'

I said, trying it out: 'Actually, I had heard of the place. I think I know some relatives of hers in England, of the old lady's. I'd thought of trying to see her. I'd wondered if perhaps I might write her a note and ask if I could visit her.' Something – I'm not quite sure what – forbade me to explain to the clerk my own relationship with his local legend.

He shook his head doubtfully, but with a gleam of curiosity in his eyes which told me that my reticence had probably been wise. 'I suppose you could try, but when she would get it, or when you would get an answer . . . There is a porter at the gate' – he shrugged – 'but they say he lets no one through at all. He takes in the supplies and pays for them, and if there are letters, or if she has written letters, they are handed over at that time. But for a long time now she has received no one – no one, that is, except the doctor.'

'The doctor? Is she ill?'

'Oh, no, not now. I believe I did hear of something last year – about six months ago, in the autumn, and the doctor going up each day. But she recovered, and now is well enough.'

She had certainly been well enough, I reflected, to draft another snappy Last Will and Testament at Christmas. 'A doctor from Beirut, was this?'

'Yes, an English doctor.'

'Do you know his name?' I added, rather apologetically: 'If I can't see her, I might get news of her from him.'

The clerk could not remember the doctor's name, but he promised to find out for me, and indeed the next time I passed the desk he had it ready, a Dr Henry Grafton with an address somewhere near Martyrs'

Square. I thanked him, and went back upstairs to my room, where I picked up the telephone directory and found Grafton, H. L.

The number was there. After a little trouble I managed to get it, and a man's voice answered in Arabic, but when we had sorted ourselves out through his excellent French into his even better English, he had to disappoint me. No, Dr Grafton was not here, Dr Grafton had left Beirut some time back. Yes, for good. If he could help me . . . ?

'I was just making some enquiries about a relation of mine,' I said, 'a Mrs. Boyd. I understand she was a patient of Dr Grafton's a few months back when he was in Beirut. I wonder – is she perhaps now on your list? The thing is—'

'Mrs. Boyd?' The voice was puzzled. 'We don't have anyone of that name, I'm afraid. What's the address?'

'She lives outside Beirut, at a place called Dar Ibrahim. I believe it's near a village called Sal'q.'

'Dar Ibrahim?' The voice quickened. 'Do you mean the Lady Harriet?'

'Why, yes, I – I suppose I do,' I said, feeling rather foolish. 'I – I'd forgotten . . . yes, of course, the Lady Harriet.'

'As far as I know she's fine,' said the voice, 'but she's certainly not my patient. In the normal way I would have attended her after Grafton left, but she wrote to tell me she had made other arrangements.' Some undercurrent, perhaps of amusement, in the smooth voice made me want to ask what these were, but this was hardly possible. Probably (I thought) a letter renouncing the world, the English, and the medical profession, or at least another Last Will and Testament. 'May I know who is calling?' asked the voice.

'Lady Harriet's great-niece. My name is Christabel Mansel. I'm here in the Lebanon on holiday, and I – none of us has heard from my great-aunt for some time; in fact, I'd got the idea she was dead. But then I heard she was still alive, and someone at the hotel here – I'm staying at the Phoenicia – told me Dr Grafton had attended her, so I thought I'd ring him up to find out anything I could. You say he's left Beirut. Is he still in the Lebanon? Would it be possible to get in touch with him?'

'I'm afraid not. He went back to London.'

'I see. Well, thanks very much, I might try to look her up myself.'

There was a slight pause at the other end. Then the voice said, carefully expressionless: 'One gathers she lives very much retired.'

'Yes,' I said, 'I understood so. But anyway, thank you for your help. Goodbye.'

'Goodbye,' said the voice.

I found myself grinning as I put the receiver down. What was implicit in the pleasant voice was, unmistakably, the Arabic equivalent for 'and the best of British luck'.

Charles rang up that evening to say that Ben's father had been delayed, so he himself couldn't get up before Sunday evening at the earliest, and might not even manage that. 'But in the name of all the gods at once,' he finished impressively, 'I'll be with you on Monday, or perish in the attempt.'

'Don't ask for it,' I said, 'at least not till you've bought your blue bead. You told me this was a country where anything could happen.'

I didn't mention my own enquiries about Great-Aunt Harriet, or that I was beginning to develop quite a lively sense of curiosity about the eccentric recluse of Dar Ibrahim.

The desk clerk had certainly done his best to get me a nice expensive trip. The car was a vast American affair with fins, air-conditioning, blue beads to ward off the Evil Eye, and hanging in the window a text from the Koran which said: 'Place your reliance on God.'

It also had an altimeter. This I didn't quite believe in until the driver, a lively sharp-faced young man called Hamid, told me we would be going from sea level to about eight thousand feet in one fell swoop, since the Adonis Source was right up in the High Lebanon. I settled down beside him in the front of the car, and watched the altimeter with fascinated amusement as we turned away from the coast at Byblos, and began to climb.

Hamid had underestimated the number of fell swoops that were required. At first the road was reasonable, and bored its way upwards through villages and terraced fields, where the carefully spaced apple trees stood knee-deep in growing crops, and dark-eyed children played among the hens in the dust. But after a while the road shook itself clear of the little green settlements to climb more steeply through the last belt of cultivation before the flocks claimed the stony earth. Here still in every sheltered corner a neat terraced wall dammed in some carefully banked soil, and fruit trees were in meagre bloom. On the more exposed terraces the thin green blades of some grain were growing, almost smothered by the sheets of spring flowers that grew everywhere, at the roadside, in the terraced walls, in the very seams of the rocks. Hamid stopped the car with smiling good nature and let me explore them with rapture; orchids, pale cyclamens, a huge flax-blue geranium, the scarlet-petalled Persian tulip, and the red anemone that flowers for Adonis.

Presently we were out of the cultivation and running along switchback ridges where grey shrubs clung to the rock, and the only flower was the yellow broom. The air was crystal clear, and in wonderful contrast to the heavy air of the coast. Now and again we saw a flock of the Eastern-looking sheep, cream or honey-coloured or spatchcocked with black, moving with drooping ears and heads carried low as if always looking for food. Glossy black goats grazed with them, and each flock bunched closely round its shepherd, a solitary figure standing wrapped in his *burnous*, arms crossed over his stick, watching gravely as we went by.

The road climbed. The altimeter needle moved steadily to the right. The air grew piercingly fresh. The yellow broom dropped below us, and at the verges of the narrow way tufts of grey, thin leaves hunched among the stones. The car swerved terrifyingly round bends with rocks threatening to scrape the offside wing, and on the other side a sheer abyss where crows and ravens tilted and croaked below us.

Then suddenly there was space on both sides. We were running along the hogsback of a dizzyingly exposed ridge with, to the left, a prospect of white rock and blue distance and crest on crest of wooded mountain to the sea; and deep down on our right, ice-green, flashing and hiding and flashing again as it rushed and curled down its great forested gorge, ran the Nahr Ibrahim, the Adonis River.

And presently, dipping through rocky gorges which trapped the sun here and there and allowed thin apple trees to blossom with their feet deep in the red anemones, we came to the Adonis Source itself.

The source of the Adonis River has been magic, time out of mind. To the primitive people of a thirsty land, the sight of that white torrent bursting straight out of its roaring black cave half up a massive, sun-baked cliff, suggested God knows what gods and demons and power and terror. It certainly suggested fertility . . . the river carries life with it for thirty water-seamed mountain miles. And where the water bursts from the rock the corrie is suddenly green, and full of trees and flowering bushes, and the red anemone grows along the torrent side.

So here, treading on the ghostly heels of Isis and Ishtar and Astarte and the Great Mother herself who was Demeter and Dia and Cybele of the towers, came Aphrodite to fall in love with the Syrian shepherd Adonis, and lie with him among the flowers. And here the wild boar killed him, and where his blood splashed, anemones grew, and to this day every spring the waters of the Adonis run red right down to the sea. Now the corrie is empty except for the black goats sleeping in the sun on the ruined floor of Aphrodite's temple, and against the roar of the torrent the drowsy stirrings of the goat bells come sharp and clear. The rags that flutter from the sacred tree are tied there as petitions to the last and latest Lady of the place, Mary.

Even without the legends, it would have been breath-taking. With them, the scene of white water and blazing rock, massive ruins, and bright flowers blowing in the wind from the fall, was something out of this world. And as we turned eventually out of the corrie on to the track – it could hardly have been called a road – that would take us home by a different route, the scene had its final touch of Eastern fantasy.

A little way beyond and out of sight of the Adonis corrie, a few Arab houses straggled along the waterside. A path, a white scratch on the rock, climbed out of this at an angle to the road. And up this path, going easily, went a chestnut Arab horse, the white *burnous* of its rider filled out by the motion like a sail, the scarlet and silver of the bridle winking in the sun. At the horse's heels cantered two beautiful dogs, fawn-coloured greyhounds with long silky hair, the saluki hounds which were used by the princes of the East for hunting gazelle.

A curve of the road hid them, and all at once it was an ordinary day again. We were at the hotel, and it was time for lunch.

We saw the rider again, on our way down the other

side of the valley. We had spent more than an hour over lunch, and the horseman must have used paths which cut off a thousand difficult corners that a car had to take. As we picked our way between the potholes into some tiny settlement in a lost high valley where the snow lay not very far above us, I saw the rider below, walking his horse down a barely visible path that took him thigh-deep through a field of sunflowers. The dogs were invisible below the thick, heart-shaped leaves. Then they raced ahead of him out on to a lower curve of the road, the horse breaking into a canter behind them. So clear was the air that I could hear the jingling of bridle bells above the thud of hoofs in the dust.

The squat peeling houses of the village crowded in on the car and hid him from view.

We stopped in the village to buy oranges.

This was Hamid's idea. We could have bought them at one of the dozens of stalls on the way out of Beirut, but these, he said, would be something special, straight from the tree and warm with the sun and ripe, divinely ripe.

'And I shall buy them for you as a present,' he said, drawing the car to a halt in the shade of a mulberry tree and coming round to open the door for me.

The village was poor, that was obvious; the houses were nothing more than shacks patched with mud brick, but they were screened with vines, and each one squatted among its laborious terraces of fruit and grain. Some of the Goddess's fertility had spilled over into the place, for all its height. It must be sheltered

from the worst of the winds, and there would be no lack
of moisture as the snow melted. The carefully trapped
water stood deep-green in square cisterns under the
bare silver poplars, and the village – just a handful of
houses in a natural amphitheatre sheltered from the
wind – was full of fruit blossom, not only the enchanting glossy trees heavy with the waxy flowers and fruit
of oranges and lemons, but the snow of pears and the
sharp pink of almond, and everywhere the blush-pink
of the apple, the staple fruit of the Lebanon.

The sun was hot. A small crowd of staring children
had gathered round the car; they were very small and
rather engaging, with their thick black hair and
enormous dark eyes and thumb-sucking curiosity.
The place seemed dead, with the afternoon deadness.
No one was in the fields; if there was a café it was only
some dark room in one of the cottages; and I saw no
women. Apart from the children, the skinny hens
scratching, and a miserable-looking donkey with rope
sores, the only creature moving was an old man who
sat in the sun smoking a pipe. He could, indeed, hardly
be said to be moving. He seemed to be smoking almost
in his sleep, and his eyes turned up slowly and half
blind to Hamid as the latter greeted him and asked him
a question in Arabic, presumably who would sell us the
fruit that hung still on the lovely trees.

The old man waited a full half minute while the
question wound its way through his brain, then he
removed the pipe from his mouth, turned his head
through a full three degrees, spat revoltingly into the
dust, and mumbled something to himself. Then his

eyes resumed their myopic staring at vacancy, and the pipe went back into his mouth.

Hamid grinned at me, shrugged, said: 'I won't be a moment,' and vanished into a dark doorway.

I wandered across the street, the children following. At the edge of the road was a six-foot retaining wall holding up, it seemed, the entire plateau on which the village was built. Below this were the terraced fields where I had seen the rider on the chestnut horse. The sunflowers were too tall and too thickly planted to allow the lovely profusion of flowers that I had seen in the lower reaches of the hills, but there were wild irises at the foot of the wall, and a blue flower like a small lily, and like shining drops of blood among the sunflower roots I could see the red anemones.

I climbed down. The children climbed down, too. I helped them, bodily lifting down the last one a half-naked atom of perhaps three, probably with scabies. I dusted my hands off on my slacks, and hunted for flowers.

The children helped. A big-eyed boy in a grubby vest and nothing else yanked out a handful of pinks for me, and little Scabies came up with a dandelion or two. There was a great deal of conversation. Arabic and English and (from Scabies) stone-age grunts, and we all understood one another very well. The clearest thing about the business was that I was expected to hand over something substantial in return for the company and the flowers.

'A shilling,' said Hamid from above me, sounding amused.

I looked up. He was standing at the edge of the road.

'Are you sure? It seems very little. There's six of them.'

'It's quite enough.'

It seemed he was right. The children grabbed the coins, and melted up and over the wall faster than they had come down and with no assistance whatever, except for Scabies, who was heaved over the last lap by Hamid, dusted off, and sent on his way with a clap over the bare buttocks. Hamid turned back to me.

'Can you manage it? Some of the stones aren't too steady.'

'I won't bother. I'll just walk down and meet you on the road as you drive down. Did you get the oranges?'

'Yes. All right, then, don't hurry, I'll wait for you below.'

The path where I had seen the rider was a dry and well-worn right of way some eighteen inches wide, going down at a slant through the sunflowers and descending by three or four stony gaps in the terracing. The huge flowers, heavy-headed, were turned away from me, facing south, and the path was a narrow chasm between head-high plants. I saw now that they were planted a yard or so apart, and between them some other plant with glaucous green leaves and plumes of brownish flowers fought its way up with mallow and cornflowers and a dozen other things towards the light. Where the horse had brushed through, the leaves hung bruised and crumpled, and above the honey-smell of the sunflowers there was the clean, musky smell of dead nettle.

I made my way down towards the road. At the gap in the wall leading down to the last terrace the sunflowers gave way to a more familiar crop of corn, and standing sentinel where the crops divided was a fig tree, its buds just bursting into young green. Its silver boughs held the buds up against the bright sky with an enchanting grace, and against the rough-cast of its stem some wild vine-like plant clung, with flowers as red as the anemones. I stopped to pick one. The vine was tough, and a hank of it pulled away from the trunk, uncovering something that lay below. On the bleached silver of the exposed stem, scrawled in red, was the sketch of a running dog. The drawing was crude but lively; the thing was unmistakably a long-haired greyhound with a plumed tail. A saluki.

It is surely common experience that when something has been brought to your attention it crops up again and again, often with an alarming appearance of co-incidence or even fate. It certainly seemed as if, once Charles had mentioned them, the creatures were going to haunt me through the Lebanon, but there was after all nothing so very odd about it; one might say that in England it is possible to be haunted by poodles, I went down to the road.

Hamid was sitting on a low wall at the edge of the road beside the car, smoking. He got up quickly, but I waved him down.

'Don't bother. Finish your cigarette, do.'

'Would you like an orange?'

'I'd love one. Thanks. Oh, aren't they gorgeous? You're quite right, we don't get them like this at home . . . Hamid, why do they grow sunflowers?'

'For oil. They make very good cooking oil, almost as good as olive oil, and now the Government has built a factory to make margarine with it also, and it offers a good price for the crop. It's part of an official campaign to stop the growing of hemp.'

'Hemp? That's hashish, isn't it? – marihuana? Good heavens! Does it grow up here?'

'Oh, yes. Have you never seen it? I believe you grow the same plant in England, to make rope, but only in hot countries does it bear the drug. In past time there has always been a lot of it grown up in the hills – it's the right climate for it, and there are still places where the inspectors don't go.'

'Inspectors?'

He nodded. 'Government officials. They're very anxious now to get the growing of these drugs under control. A certain amount is grown legally, you understand, for medical use, and for every stage of its growth and handling you must have a licence and be subjected to strict controls, but it's always been easy enough for the peasants in these wild parts to grow more than they declare, or to harvest the crop before the inspectors come. Now the penalties have been made stricter than ever, but there are still some who try to get past the law.' He lifted his shoulders. 'What would you? It pays, and there are always men who will take the big risks for the big money.' He dropped his cigarette into the road and trod the butt into the dust. 'You saw the old man up there, the one I spoke to?'

'Yes.'

'He was smoking it.'

'But can he . . . ? I mean—'

'How can they stop him?'

I stared. 'Do you mean it's grown here?'

He smiled. 'There was some growing beside his house among the potatoes.'

'I wouldn't know it if I saw it,' I said. 'What's it look like?'

'A tall plant, greyish colour, not very pretty. The drug comes from the flowers. These are brownish, a spike like soft feathers.'

I had been carefully depositing my orange peel out of sight behind the wall where we sat. Now I sat bolt-upright. 'There was something like that growing under the sunflowers!'

'So?' he said indifferently. 'It will be gone before the inspectors get here. Shall we go?' He opened the car door for me.

All in all it had been a strange and heady sort of day. And things seemed to be going my way. It seemed the inevitable climax to it that as I got into the car I should say with decision:

'You said you'd show me Dar Ibrahim on the way home. If there's time, I think I'd like to call there today. Would you mind?'

At about four o'clock we slid round a steep bend and into the village of Sal'q. Hamid stopped the car beside a low wall beyond which the land dropped clear away to give another of those staggering views of the Adonis Valley.

'There,' he said.

I looked where he pointed. Here the valley was wide, with the river, magnificent and flowing swiftly, cutting a way down for itself between dense banks of trees. From somewhere to our left, beyond the little village mosque, fell the tributary river to meet the Adonis in the valley at the bottom. Between the two streams a highish, wedge-shaped tongue of land thrust out like a high-prowed ship down the valley's centre, and on its tip, like a crown on the crag above the meeting waters, sprawled the palace, a seemingly vast collection of buildings running back from the edge of the promontory to spread over a fair area of the plateau. Towards the rear of the buildings the ground fell away sharply in a small escarpment shelving down to the level of the plateau, and here the palace wall rose straight out of the rock. Near the top I could see windows, a row of ornate arches looking out towards the village, but apart from these, except for a few small, square openings that seemed to be little more than ventilators, the walls were windowless, blank and white in the sun. Towards the back of the palace the green of sizable trees showed inside the walls. Outside, stretching back towards the roots of the mountains that divided the gorges of the Adonis and its tributary, the plateau stretched open and stony and barren as the valley of dry bones.

There seemed to be no way to get there except down a rocky track along the side of the tributary stream.

This Hamid was explaining. 'And you have to cross the water at the bottom,' he said. 'There is a ford with shallow water, but sometimes in the spring, you understand, when there has been rain, it can be very deep and fast, and floods over the stepping-stones. But it will be all right today. You really wish to go? Then I will come with you to show you the way.'

It did not seem to me that it would be very easy to miss the way. I could see the path as far as the bottom of the hill, and – I am very long-sighted – I could even see the ford from where I stood. There must have been a stone bridge there at one time, for the ruined piles were unmistakable. And no doubt beyond that the track up to the palace would be equally unmistakable.

I looked at Hamid in his immaculately pressed dark city trousers and equally immaculate shirt.

'That's very good of you, but there's no need for you to bother, you know. I can hardly miss the way. If you'd rather stay here with the car, and perhaps find something to drink in the village, some coffee, perhaps, if there's a café . . . ?' I looked round me at the singularly unpromising gaggle of huts which was the village of Sal'q.

He grinned. 'There is, but with all gratitude, I shall not try it today. I will certainly come down with you. It's a long way for a lady to go alone, and besides, I believe that the porter there speaks nothing but Arabic. You would perhaps find it a little difficult to make yourself sufficiently understood?'

'Oh, lord, yes, I suppose so. Well, thanks very much, I'd be terribly grateful if you'd come. It looks a pretty tough walk, I must say. I wish we had wings.'

He locked the car, and dropped the key into his pocket. 'Along here.'

The path led round the wall of the mosque, past the

little graveyard with its curious Moslem stones; the slender pillars with their stone turbans which indicated the graves of men, the lotus-carved steles for the women. The whitewashed minaret stood prettily against the pale hot sky. Past the crumbling corner of the graveyard wall the track suddenly turned down-hill in steep zigzags, treacherous with loose stones. The sun was heeling over from its zenith, but still beat fiercely on this side of the valley. Soon we had gone below the lowest of the village terraces, where the hillside was too steep and too stony for anything, even vines, to grow. Some bluff of hot rock hid the stream from us, so that no sound of it came to our ears. The silence was intense. The whole width of the valley seemed to be filled with the same hot, dry silence.

Round a steep turn in the path we disturbed a herd of goats, black and brown with long silky hair, flop ears, huge horns and sleepy, wicked yellow eyes. They had been grazing on heaven knows what on that barren slope, and now slept in the sun. There were about thirty of them, their narrow clever faces – watching us with calculation and without a hint of fear – giving the impression somehow not that this was a herd of animals owned by men, but that we were walking through a colony of creatures who lived here by right. When one of them got leisurely to its feet and strolled into the middle of the path, I didn't argue with it. I got off the path and walked round it. It didn't even turn its head.

I had been right about the old bridge. The tributary (Hamid told me it was called the Nahr el-Sal'q) was

not wide compared to the Adonis, but at this time of
year there was fully twenty feet of it to cross, swiftly
sliding water, shallow in places over white pebbles, in
others tumbling with foam over split boulders, or
whirling deeper in a hard dark green in pools which
must have been breast deep. At the far side the water
was bounded by a low cliff, perhaps five feet high, from
which the bridge had originally sprung. The foun-
dations could be seen deep in the clear water. On
the side where we stood there was little left but a pile of
large squared stones, some of which had been removed
and roughly arranged in the water to make stepping-
stones about a yard apart.

'There was an old bridge here once, a Roman bridge,
they say,' said Hamid. 'These are still the old stones.
Can you manage it?'

He took my hand to help me across, then led the way
straight for the foot of the cliff, where I saw a path
curling its way up through tangles of wild fig and
yellow broom towards the head of the promontory.

It was a steep climb but not difficult, obviously
practicable for mules or even horses. We saw no sign
of life other than the lizards, and the kestrels which
circled above the cliff. There was no sound except that
of the water running below us, and the scrape of our
steps, and our breathing.

As we came out eventually at the top of the crag and
saw the eyeless walls of the palace in front of us, I had
the oddest feeling that the building was completely
dead and deserted, that this was almost a place outside
life. It seemed impossible that anyone should live there,

least of all anyone I had known. No one, surely, who had ever been a part of my own extraordinary but vital family could shut themselves away here in this bone-white graveyard of a place . . .

As I paused to get my breath, eyeing the scoured pale walls, the locked gate of bronze, I found myself remembering the last time I had seen Great-Aunt Harriet. It was a dim childhood's memory . . . The orchard at home, at windfall time, and one of those soft gusty September winds with the leaves swirling, and the apples thudding into the damp turf. The sky was full of afternoon clouds, and the rooks wheeling to go home. I remembered Great-Aunt Harriet's voice cawing like a rook with laughter at something Charles had said . . .

'There used to be a bell beside the door. You tell me what you want me to say, and if the old chap isn't asleep, we might get him to take a message,' said Hamid cheerfully, leading the way across the dusty rock towards the gate.

3

This batter'd Caravanserai . . .
E. FitzGerald: *The Rubáiyát of*
Omar Khayyám of Naîshápûr

THE main gate – double leaves of studded bronze
under an elaborately carved arch – was at first sight
vastly impressive, but as one approached it could be
seen that the heavy knocker had vanished from its
hinge and that the carving had been fretted almost to
nothing by the wind. The walls, high and blind,
showed here and there the remains of some coloured
decoration, ghostly patterns and mosaics and broken
marble plastered over and painted a pale ochre colour
which had baked white with the strong sunlight. There
was a bell pull to the right-hand side of the gate.

Hamid tugged the handle. Distinctly, in the silence,
we could hear the creak of the wires as they strained,
foot by rusty foot, to pull the bell. Seconds later, with a
squeak and jangle of springs, it clanged hollowly just
inside the gate. As the echo ran humming down the
bronze a dog barked somewhere. After that, again,
there was silence.

Hamid had just raised his hand again to the bell

when we heard footsteps. Hardly footsteps; just the whispering shuffle of slippers on a dusty floor, then the sound of hands fumbling at the other side of the gate. It was no surprise to hear the heavy sound of bolts being dragged back, or that, when the gate began to open, it creaked ominously.

I caught Hamid's eye, and saw in it the same bright anticipation as was no doubt in my own. After such a build-up, whoever opened the gate to us could hardly fail to be an anticlimax.

But he wasn't. He was better than all expectation. One tall leaf of bronze creaked slowly open on a passage that seemed, in contrast to the sunlight where we stood, to be quite dark. In the cautious crack that had opened we could see a thin bent figure robed in white. For one mad moment – such had been the Hitchcock lead in to his appearance – I thought the man had no face; then I saw that he was dark, almost black, and against the blackness of the passage behind him only his white robes showed up.

He peered out into the light, an oldish man, stoop-shouldered, his skin wrinkled like a prune under the folds of the *kaffiyeh*, or Arab head-dress. His eyes, red-rimmed and puckered against the light, had a greyish look about them which spoke of cataract. He blinked, mouthed something at Hamid which I took to be Arabic, and started to shut the gate.

'One moment. Wait.' Hamid was past me into the gap with one quick stride, and had a tough young shoulder against the gate. He had already told me what he intended to say. The quickfire Arabic sounded urgent. 'This is no ordinary visitor, but one of your Lady's family, whom you cannot turn from the door. Listen.'

The old man paused uncertainly, and Hamid went on. 'My name is Hamid Khalil, from Beirut, and I have driven this young lady up to see your mistress. Now, we know your Lady receives no visitors, but this young lady is English, and she is the daughter of the Lady's brother's son. So you must go and see your Lady and tell her that Miss Christy Mansel has come from England to see her – Miss Christy Mansel, bearing greetings from all the Lady's relatives in England.'

The porter was staring, stupidly, almost as if he had not heard. I began to wonder if he were deaf. Then I saw he was looking at me, and that in the opaque eyes a sort of curiosity was stirring. But he shook his head, and again from his lips came those strangled sounds which I realised now were the struggles of someone with a severe speech impediment.

Hamid shrugged at me, expressively. 'They didn't tell us the half, did they? "No communication with outside" is right – this man's all but dumb. However, I don't think he's deaf, so I dare say he has some way of taking messages. There's no need yet for despair.'

'That wasn't quite what I was feeling.'

He laughed and turned back to the old man, who, gobbling and muttering under his breath, had been making vague attempts to shut the door against the younger man's determined shoulder and (by now) foot. Hamid raised his voice and spoke again, sharply.

Even without his subsequent translation to me, the gist of what he said was obvious.

'Look, stop that, you understand me quite well, don't pretend that you don't, so stop playing about with the gate, we're not going away until you've taken the message to your mistress, or sent someone who can talk to us . . . That's better! Now, have you got it? Miss Christy Mansel, daughter of her brother's son, has come from England to see her, even just for a few moments. Is that clear? Now go and give the message.'

There was no doubt that the old man could hear. Open curiosity showed now in the face that shot forward on its stringy neck to stare at me, but he still made no attempt to go, or to invite us in. He shook his head violently, mouthing at Hamid and holding on to the edge of the gate with what looked like a mixture of obstinacy and apprehension.

I intervened, half uneasy, half repelled: 'Look, Hamid, perhaps we shouldn't. I mean, forcing our way in like this . . . He's obviously had his orders, and he looks scared to death at having to disobey them. Perhaps if I just write a note—'

'If we go away now you'll never get in. It's not your great-aunt he's scared of. As far as I can make out he's saying something about a doctor, "The doctor says no one is to go in".'

'The *doctor*?'

'Don't worry,' he said quickly, 'I may be wrong, I can hardly make him out, but I thought that's what he said. Wait a minute . . .'

Another spate of Arabic, and again the horrible

stammering syllables from the old man. Flakes of spittle had appeared at the corners of his mouth, and he shook his head violently, and even partially loosed his panic hold of the door to flap his hands at us like someone driving hens.

'Please—' I said.

Hamid silenced the old man with a snapped word and a gesture. 'Yes?'

'Hamid,' I said decisively, 'this settles it, I insist on getting in. If I can't see my great-aunt, I'll see the doctor, if he's here. If he isn't, then someone must write his name and address down for me, and I'll go and see him straight away. Tell him that. Tell him I insist. And if you like you can tell him that my family can make quite a bit of trouble if anything should happen to my great-aunt, and the family not be allowed to know about it.' I added: 'And for pity's sake if there's anyone at all in the place who *can* talk to us, we want to see them, and fast.'

'I'll tell him.'

How he did actually express my demands I have no idea, but after a further few minutes of wrangling the porter, filmed eyes turned up hideously to heaven and palms thrown up to disclaim all responsibility, pulled open the door at last and let us through.

Hamid gave the ghost of a wink at me as he stood back to let me pass him. 'I told him you were exhausted with the walk from Sal'q and refused to wait outside in the sun. If we'd once let him shut the door I doubt if we'd ever have heard from him again.'

'I'm sure we wouldn't. For goodness' sake come

with me, won't you? I mean, something tells me I may not be welcome.'

'I wouldn't leave you for worlds,' said Hamid comfortably, taking me by the elbow to steer me into the cool darkness. 'I only hope that you find all is well with the Lady . . . and I may easily have been mistaken in what that old dervish was trying to say. Well, at least we are inside . . . That alone is something to tell my children's children.'

Behind us the gate creaked shut, and there were the ominous sounds of the bolts being replaced. As my eyes adjusted themselves to the dimness I saw that we were not actually in a passage, but in a high barrel-roofed tunnel about fifteen feet long which ended in another heavy door. To either side of the tunnel was a smaller door. One of these was open, and in the dim light of a slit window in the inner wall I saw an ancient truckle-bed covered with tumbled blankets. The porter's lodge, no doubt; perhaps originally a guardroom. The door opposite this was shut.

The old man opened the door at the tunnel's end, letting in a shaft of bright light. We followed him into a big courtyard.

This would be the outer court of the original palace; the *midan*, where the Emir's people would gather with gifts or petitions, and where his troops would show off their horsemanship with games and mock fights, or ride in to dismount after battle or the hunt. Under the archways on three sides were buildings which must have been stables and harness rooms and perhaps quarters for soldiers; on the fourth, to our left as we entered, was a high wall beyond which I saw a glimpse of green. In its heyday, with the bustle of servants and the tramp of horses and rattle of arms, it would have been an impressive place. Now it was quiet and empty, but the scuffed dust showed recent evidence of beasts, and the place smelled of horses.

The porter did not pause here, but led us right-handed across the *midan* and in under the arcade, through another door which gave on a darkened passage. Through this his white robes shuffled dimly ahead. Vaguely I glimpsed passages going off to the left and right, and doors, some of them open on rooms where it was too dark to see anything; but in one of these some kind of skylight shed a glimmer on sacks and boxes and a stack of broken chairs. The passage took three right-angled turns through this labyrinth before it led us out into another courtyard, this time small, and little more than a light-well lined with arched grilles, and one blind wall against which was piled a stack of timber. As we passed I saw out of the corner of my eye a streak of movement which, when I looked sharply that way, had ceased. Nothing. But I knew it had been a rat.

Another corridor; more doors, some of them open and giving on dilapidated and dirty rooms. The whole place had the air of something deserted long since, and lived in only by rats and mice and spiders. Not a floor but was filthy, with gaps in the ornamental tiling; the wall mosaics were dim and battered, the window grilles broken, the lintels cracked. A heavy, dusty silence slept over everything like a grey blanket. I remember that as we passed some crumbling wall a rusty nail fell from its socket with a clink that made me jump, and the rustle of plaster falling after it sounded like a puff of wind in dry leaves.

It was a far cry from the 'enchanted palace' that imagination – more powerful than reason – had led me to expect. I began to wonder with tightening nerves what I should find at the end of this quest. 'Stark raving bonkers' had been Charles's verdict, and had seemed, as he delivered it, no more than faintly comic; but here, following the shuffling guide along yet another corridor with its dim and dwindling prospect of warped and gaping doors, its uneven floorings, its smell of years-old decay, I began, quite fervently, to wish I had not come. The thought of coming face to face with the combination of helplessness, senility, and perhaps sickness, which must live at the centre of all this decay like a spider in the middle of an old dusty cobweb, could fill me with nothing but dismay.

Suddenly we were out into another courtyard. I had completely lost my bearings by this time, but from the fact that beyond the roofs on the far side I could see crests of feathery green, I guessed we were somewhere towards the back of the palace.

This court was about fifty feet square, and at one time must have been as ornamental as the one where Charles and I had talked in Damascus; but now, like all else, it had fallen into disrepair. In its better days it had been floored with marble, with blue tiled arcades and pretty pillars and a pool at the centre. At the foot of each pillar stood a carved marble trough for flowering plants. These were still full of soil, but now held only grass and some tightly clenched, greyish-looking buds. There was one spindly tamarisk hanging over the broken coping of the pool. Somewhere, a cicada purred gently. Grey thistles grew in the gaps of the pavement, and the pool was dry.

Under the arcade to one side was the usual deep alcove in the shadow where, up a single step, was the dais with seats on three sides. I would have distrusted any cushions that this place might produce, but I need not have worried; the seats were of unpadded marble. Here the porter indicated that we should sit, then, with another grotesque bout of yammering directed at Hamid, he turned and went. Silence came back, broken only by the churring of the cicada.

'Smoke?' asked Hamid, producing cigarettes. He lit mine for me and then wandered back into the sunlight of the courtyard, where he squatted down with his back against a pillar, absently narrowing his eyes against the brilliant sky where the trees beyond the wall waved their green feathers.

'If she does not receive you, what will you do?'

'Go away, I suppose, once I've seen the doctor.'

He turned his head. 'I am sorry. You are distressed.'

I hesitated. 'Not really. I hardly know her, and I'm pretty sure she won't remember me. She spent most of her time out East till her husband died, and after that she only lived in England for about two years – that was when I was very small. She left fifteen years ago, for good, when I was seven. I haven't seen her since the time she came to say goodbye. I'd hardly be surprised if she just sent a message back now to say she can't even remember my name. That is, if the dervish gets it right . . . I wonder if he can give a message at all? As a non-communicator he just about wins, wouldn't you say? He ought to be at the Royal Court.'

'But surely your Queen would not—? Ah, here he is,' said Hamid, rising, 'and praise be to Allah, he has brought someone with him.'

The 'someone' was a young man, a European, tall and thin and carelessly dressed, with light hair bleached to fair by the sun, and grey eyes. He had the slightly confused air of someone startled awake from sleep, and I suddenly remembered Great-Aunt Harriet's alleged nocturnal habits. Perhaps the staff slept during daylight? He paused for a moment in the shadow before dismissing the porter with a gesture, then came forward into the sun. I saw him wince as if its fierce light worried him, as he approached slowly and with apparent reluctance over the broken pavement. He looked about twenty-four.

His voice was friendly enough, and what was more, English.

'Good afternoon. I'm afraid I didn't get your name. I gather from Jassim that you have an urgent message for Lady Harriet? Perhaps you could give your message to me?'

'You're English? Oh, good.' I stood up. 'It's not exactly a message. My name's Mansel, Christy Mansel, and Mrs. Boyd – "Lady Harriet" – is my great-aunt. I'm in Beirut on holiday, and someone told me that my great-aunt was still living up here at Dar

Ibrahim, so I came up to see her. I'm sure my people at home will be very glad to have news of her, so if she'll spare me even a few minutes, I'd be very pleased.'

He looked surprised, and, I thought, guarded. 'A great-niece? Christy, did you say? She never mentioned anyone of that name to me.'

'Shoud she have?' My voice was perhaps a little tart. 'And you, Mr—er . . . ? I take it you live here?'

'Yes. My name's Lethman, John Lethman. I – you might say I look after your great-aunt.'

'You mean you're the doctor?'

I must have sounded a brupt and surprised, because he looked rather taken a back. 'I beg your pardon?'

'I'm sorry, it was only because I suppose you look – I mean, I expected somebody older. The porter told my driver that "the doctor" wouldn't allow anyone to see my great-aunt, that's how I knew you were here. If he did mean you, that is?'

'I suppose he did . . .' He pressed the heel of his hand to his brow, shook his head sharply as if to wake himself up, and gave me the flash of an embarrassed smile. His eyes still looked blurred and unfocused. They were grey, with wide, myopic-looking pupils. 'I'm sorry, I'm still a bit stupid, I was asleep.'

'Oh, goodness, I do apologise. When one's madly sightseeing all day one tends to forget the siesta habit . . . *I'm* sorry, Mr Lethman. It was just that when the porter said "the doctor" was here I began to think my great-aunt must be ill. I mean – if you have to live here . . . ?'

'Look,' he said, 'we'd better clear this up. I'm not a

doctor really, unless you like to count half a course in psychological medicine—' A quick look. 'And don't let that worry you, either, because I'm certainly not here in that capacity! Your great-aunt's pretty fit, and all I actually do is keep an eye on the Arab servants and see to things generally, and provide her with a bit of company and conversation. I don't "have" to live here at all in the sense you mean. All that happened was that I came here – to the Lebanon – to do some research for a paper I wanted to write, and I was marooned up here one day, driven to ground by one of the flash storms they have occasionally, and your great-aunt took me in, and somehow one thing led to another, and I stayed.' His smile had something tentative about it, but oddly disarming, so that I thought I could supply the missing bits of the story quite easily. He added: 'If you can think of a better place to write in, just tell me.'

I could think of a million better places to write in, among them almost any room almost anywhere within daily reach of people, but I didn't say so. I asked: 'How long have you been here?'

'Nearly a year. I came last July.'

'I see. Well, it's a relief to know she's all right. So I'll be able to see her?'

He hesitated, apparently on the brink of saying something, then gave that odd little shake of the head again, and ran his hand back over his brow, almost as if he were smoothing away some physical discomfort like a headache. I saw Hamid watching him curiously.

'Look,' I said, 'if you've something to tell me, go ahead. But let's sit down, shall we?'

He followed me into the shade of the divan, and we sat down. I laced my fingers round one knee and turned to regard him. He still looked uncomfortable, though not in the physical sense; his long body looked relaxed enough, and his hands were slack on his knees. But there was a tight knot of worry between his brows.

'How long since you heard from your great-aunt?' he asked at length.

'If you mean how long since I myself did, I never have. In fact I only remember seeing her about three times in my life, and the last time was when I was about seven, but my family hears from her now and again. There was a letter last year some time – just before Christmas, I think it was. She certainly wrote as if she were fairly fit and in her right – that is, fairly fit, But it didn't bother much with news.'

I got the idea that he knew what I meant, but he didn't smile. He was frowning down at his hands. 'I only asked because—' A pause, then he looked up suddenly. 'Miss Mansel, how much do you and your family know about the way she lives here?'

'I suppose we know very little, except the obvious things, that she's perhaps getting a bit more eccentric as she gets older, and that she's made her life out here for so long that it isn't very likely she'll ever want to move and come home again. You'll have gathered that our family's never been very strong on family ties and all that, and of course lately Great-Aunt Harriet's had this thing about cutting all her ties with England home and beauty – that's almost all her letters have been about, when she wrote at all. Don't think the family minded, they didn't. What she does is her own affair. But since I came out here I've heard a bit more about her, and I gather that now it's a pretty far-out kind of eccentricity . . . I mean, all this Lady Hester Stanhope imitation. Is it really true? Does she really live like that? Mr Lethman, she isn't really bats, is she?'

'No, oh no,' he said quickly. He was looking immensely relieved. 'I wondered if you knew about that. It wouldn't be very easy to start explaining from scratch, but if you know the Stanhope story it makes it relatively simple. I won't say your great-aunt deliberately set out to be a modern "Lady of the Lebanon", but when she first settled here at Dar Ibrahim she did keep a bit of state, and various people made the comparison to her, and then she discovered that the old Stanhope legend was still very much alive among the country Arabs, and she herself got a good deal of benefit from it in the way of service and influence and – you know, the various by-products of celebrity. It was the locals who started calling her "Lady Harriet", and it simply stuck. Your great-aunt was amused at first, I gather, and then she discovered it suited her to be a "character", and in the way these things have, it gradually grew beyond the point where it could be stopped, and certainly beyond the point where she could treat it as a joke, even to herself. I don't know if you can understand this?'

'I think so,' I said. 'She couldn't detach herself any more, so she simply went with it.'

'That's it. Nor did she want to detach herself. She'd lived out here for so long, and in a way she'd made it her country, and in a curious way I believe she feels she has a kind of right to the legend.' He smiled, the first smile of genuine amusement. 'If you want the truth I think she has a fair amount in common with her original. Well, she simply settled down to enjoy it, and took a great deal of pleasure from the more picturesque details – riding out with the hounds and hawks, for instance, letting Dar Ibrahim be used again as a halt for caravans on their way from High Lebanon and Antilebanon to the sea, and receiving the occasional "distinguished traveller" – mostly archaeologists, I believe, who'd known her husband and his work. She even meddled a bit with politics, and for some time now she's been threatening – though I think it's only window-dressing myself – to turn Muslim.' He paused. 'And then of course when I turned up out of the blue she was delighted. I was to be the "resident physician" who has such a large part in the Stanhope story . . . you know that Lady Hester Stanhope kept her own doctor with her at Djoun? Well, when our "Lady Harriet" took me in, and found I'd been halfway to a medical degree, it suited her down to the ground. So I get a courtesy title which impresses the Arab servants, and what I actually do is provide your great-aunt with company and conversation. I need hardly add that if she did need medical attention I'd get it from Beirut.'

'Who does she have now that Dr Grafton's gone?'

'Dr Grafton?' He sounded quite blank, and I looked at him in surprise.

'Yes, don't you know him? Surely, if he attended her six months ago you must have been here.'

'Oh, yes, I was, I was only wondering how you knew the name.'

'Someone at the hotel who told me about Dar Ibrahim said my aunt had been ill last autumn, so I got them to find out who her doctor was, and rang him up to ask about her. I was told then that he'd left Beirut. Who does she have now?'

'She hasn't needed anyone since then, I'm glad to say. She's got a bit of a thing now about the Beirut doctors, but I've no doubt that if it's necessary I'll make her see the light.' He smiled. 'Don't worry . . . I really do look after her quite well, you know, and I run the place for her as far as one can. And if you're thinking about the general four-star-hotel atmosphere you've seen up to now, let me tell you that there are five courtyards, two gardens, three Turkish baths, a mosque, stabling for fifty horses and twelve camels, several miles of corridors including a secret passage or two, and as for mere rooms, I've never managed to count them. I use radar to get from the Prince's Court to the Seraglio.'

I laughed: 'I'm sorry, was I looking at the dust on the floor? Don't you have slaves to go with the décor?'

'Only myself and three others – Jassim the porter, a girl called Halide, and Halide's brother Nasirulla, who lives in the village and comes over during the day. Actually we manage quite well, because the old lady herself lives very simply now. I may tell you that her part of the palace is a bit better kept than this. Halide's a good girl, and looks after your aunt pretty well. You really have no need to worry about her.'

'Did I say I was worrying? I didn't mean to throw you on the defensive like this, what have I said? I'm sure Aunt Harriet's having a whale of a time being Lady of the Lebanon, and I'm glad you're here to look after her. All I want is to see her for five minutes so's I can tell my people all about it.'

Another of those pauses. Here we were, I thought; back to Square One.

He shifted on the hard seat, and glanced sideways at me.

'Yes, well, that's rather it, don't you see? The point is, we've standing orders to stall everybody off, and' – his gaze dropped again to his hands – 'anything she's ever told me about her family didn't lead me to think she'd make an exception there.'

I grinned. 'Fair enough, I'm not blaming you, or her either. But can't we let her decide for herself? I take it she doesn't know I'm here yet? Or will Jassim have got that across to her?'

'He hasn't seen her yet, he came straight to me. As a matter of fact, he gets more across than you'd think, but he didn't get your name. I wasn't sure who you were myself, till I spoke to you. I admit he isn't so hot as a messenger – you might call him one of your aunt's charities, like me – but he's pretty useful as a staller-off at the gate, and we can't get anyone much to stay here nowadays. There isn't much money, you know.'

There was something about the way he said this, looking at me steadily with those curiously unfocused eyes. I noticed that the whites were bloodshot, and he looked as if he didn't get enough sleep, but he seemed

relaxed enough now, his long spare frame slack on the
marble seat as if this were thick with silk cushions and
Persian rugs. He was dressed in grey lightweight trousers and a blue beach shirt, neither of them expensive,
but he wore on his wrist a really magnificent gold
watch, bought no doubt in Beirut. I found myself
remembering what Charles had said about Great-Aunt
Harriet's penchant for young men, and some other
corner of my mind came up with the phrase 'undue
influence'. But this I ignored; it was after all irrelevant.
If Aunt H. could get a young man to run her ram-
shackle palace for her and give her the kind of company she liked, so much the better. Especially if it was
true that there was very little money left. I wondered
just how true this was, and if Mr Lethman looked on
the sudden interruption of a relative as a threat to his
own position *vis-à-vis* the 'Lady Harriet'. In which case
my good-looking cousin Charles might be even less
welcome than I. I decided not to mention Charles till I
saw Aunt H. herself.

John Lethman was saying 'Jassim wouldn't have
been able to see your aunt yet, in any case. She usually
sleeps a good deal during the day. She's a nightbird,
you know, like her original. So if you could wait a little
longer, then I can go and ask her about it? Halide
usually goes in to wake her at about six.'

'Of course I'll wait,' I said. 'That is, if you don't
mind, Hamid?'

'Not at all,' said Hamid without moving.

There was a slight pause. Lethman glanced from
Hamid to me and back, then consulted his watch.

'Well, that's fine, it won't be long now, and we'll see.'
Another pause. He cleared his throat. 'I suppose I
ought to warn you . . . Of course I'll do all I can,
but I can't guarantee anything. She's old, and sometimes forgetful, and – well, let's call it "difficult". And
some days are worse than others.'

'And today's been a bad one?'

He made a rueful mouth. 'Not too good.'

'Well, if she really doesn't feel up to seeing me,
then that's that, isn't it? But tell her I'll come back any
time she says, when she's feeling better. I'm in Beirut
till at least mid-week, and I could stay on. I was going
to ring up soon to tell my people what I was planning,
and it'd be rather nice if I could give them news of
her. In fact, Daddy might just be ringing up himself
this evening.'

' "This evening"? Hadn't you understood? I meant
it literally when I said she was a nightbird. She usually
seems to wake up and be at her best at something
between ten and midnight, and after that she's quite
often up all night. If she receives anyone at all, that's
when she sees them.'

'Good heavens, she does play it for real, doesn't she?
Do you mean that if I'm to see her, I've got to my stay
here all night?'

'Until pretty late, at all events. Could you?'

'I could, but I can hardly keep my driver here until
the early hours of the morning. Could you put me up?
Have you a room?' I meant 'a room that's fit to sleep
in', so the question wasn't as absurd as it might have
sounded. Mr Lethman seemed to be considering the

question on its merits. There was a short pause, then he
said, agreeably enough:

'We could certainly find you one.'

I looked across at Hamid. 'Do you mind? We can
see what my great-aunt has to say, and if I do have to
wait and see her later on, would you go back without
me? You could call at the hotel and tell them I'm
having to stay up here for the night, and – are you free
tomorrow?'

'For you, yes.'

'You're very good,' I said gratefully, 'thank you. In
that case, could you come for me again in the morning?
Wait in the village, don't bother to come right across as
far as the gate.'

'I will certainly come to the gate,' said Hamid. 'Don't
you worry about that. But I don't much like going away
now and leaving you here.'

'I'll be all right. And I simply must see my great-
aunt.'

'Of course you must, this I understand. I am sorry, I
know it's none of my affair, but surely it could be
arranged that she could see you for a few minutes now,
and then I could take you back to your hotel.'

Beside me, Mr Lethman straightened suddenly. His
voice held a weariness and exasperation that was quite
obviously genuine. 'Look, I'm sorry about all this. I'm
not making this difficult just for fun, you know, in fact
I'm hating the position I seem to have got myself into,
having to stall you off when you must think I've no
standing in the matter at all—'

'I wasn't exactly thinking that,' I said, 'and you have

got standing, haven't you? I mean, this is her home, and if she's asked you to live here, there it is, and no arguments. Even if you're not officially her doctor, I suppose you could call yourself her steward or something.'

'Malvolio in person, yellow stockings, cross garters, and all.' A flick of feeling in his voice that I didn't like, gone as soon as heard. He followed it with another of those disarming smiles. 'But you see the situation's hardly normal in any way at all. I suppose I've got used to it, and in any case this is a damned queer country where one learns to accept almost anything, but I realise this place must seem pretty weird to anyone like yourself coming into it for the first time. It did to me when she first received me. She uses what were the Emir's rooms – the Prince's Court, we call it – and an old State Divan is her bedroom. It's kept pitch dark most of the time. The Stanhope woman did the same out of vanity. I don't know what your great-aunt's motive is, certainly not that, possibly just imitation; but I remember when I was taken along there at midnight the first time I wondered what sort of loony-bin I'd landed into. And lately she's taken to—' He stopped, and seemed to be examining the tip of one shoe with great attention. 'How well do you remember your great-aunt?'

'Not really at all. My impression is that she was tall and dark and had piercing black eyes and wore black, things that flew round her like the White Queen's shawl. She did have a shawl, and she used to pin it with a diamond pin. I remember Mummy saying that her diamonds were filthy. That struck me as funny, I don't know why.'

'Diamonds? I'm afraid they must have gone long since. I never saw any.' He sounded regretful, I thought. 'Actually she's not so very tall, though I suppose she'd seem so to a child. And as for her clothes now, they're part of the legend, too.'

'Oh, I know, she dresses like an Eastern male. Well, why not?' I unclasped my hands from my knees and straightened a trouser leg. 'I dress like a European one, after all.'

'I wasn't fooled,' said Mr Lethman, with the first really human glimmer he had shown. The worried look had lightened a little. He got to his feet. 'Well, I'll go and see what the score is. I'll certainly try to persuade her to see you straight away. It's possible she may, and welcome you with open arms, but if she won't, we can make arrangements for you to stay the night. All right?'

'All right.'

'That's fine, then. I'll let you know the worst.'

He smiled perfunctorily and left us.

I went over to the pool and sat down on the coping beside Hamid.

'Did you hear all that?'

'Most of it,' said Hamid. 'What you might call a funny setup, eh? Smoke?'

'Not just now, thanks. I don't very often, actually.'

'He does.'

'How d'you mean?'

'Hashish.'

I stared. 'No? Does he? How do you know?'

He lifted his shoulders. 'His eyes, didn't you notice? And other signs – one gets to know them. He'd been smoking when we came.'

'Then that's why he was so sleepy and other-worldly! He said he'd been asleep, and let me think it was just a siesta. I thought he'd probably been up part of the night with my great-aunt. Smoking! No wonder he resented being interrupted!'

'I don't suppose he was resenting you. The smoke can make you relaxed and easy-going, and not know what you're doing. He was finding it hard to think. I smoke it myself sometimes; everybody does in the Lebanon.'

'*Do* you?'

He smiled. 'Not when I'm driving, don't worry. And not much, me; I've too much sense, and it's dangerous. It affects different people different ways, and by the time you've found what it does to you, sometimes it is too late. Did you hear him say he was writing a book? If he stays here and smokes *marjoun*, he will never write it. He will think for years that he has only to start tomorrow, and it will be the best book ever written . . . but he will never start. This is what the *marjoun* does; it gives you visions and takes away the will to translate them. He will end up like that old man, coughing in the sun and dreaming dreams . . . What will you do if he comes back to say the old lady won't see you at all?'

'I don't quite know.'

'I'll tell you what I should do. If he says she will not see you, tell him that you wish to hear this from the old lady herself. If he will not allow this, then tell him that you can only accept such an order from a real doctor, and that you wish a doctor from Beirut to see her straight away. Oh, you can do this very pleasantly. Ask him which doctor he recommends, and what time tomorrow will be convenient. Then you tell me, and I bring you.'

There wasn't much expression in his voice, but I stared at him. 'What are you suggesting?'

'Nothing.' He shrugged again. 'Seems to me that things must go very much as he orders them here, and we only have his word for it that there is no money left. She was – I repeat was – a very rich old lady.'

'But the family don't care about—' I stopped. It was patently no use explaining to Hamid that nobody wanted Great-Aunt Harriet to do anything with her own money except have a good time on her own terms. Anyway, there were other considerations here than money. I said, slowly: 'If it's true that she's perfectly fit, I'd say she can probably take care of herself, and I'm also pretty sure she wouldn't thank me for inter-fering. All I want is to know that she is still "hale and hearty", and that being so she can dispose of her filthy old diamonds any way she pleases. He's probably right that she's done it already.'

'Very likely.' I didn't know whether Hamid's dry tone meant that he was thinking of the economies obviously practised in the palace, or of John Lethman's gold wristwatch. He added: 'I do not suggest anything, me, but I have a very unpleasant nature.'

'So have I. And if he really is smoking marihuana – hashish, that is—' I took a breath. 'That settles it. I shall insist, whatever he says. I'm terribly sorry to have kept you hanging about like this, you've been very patient.'

'You are paying for my car for the day, and for my time. How I spend the time is no matter, and it saves petrol to sit in the sun and smoke.'

I laughed. 'You got something there. And you're right, I must see her. If necessary I shall play hell and insist.'

'There's no need.'

I jumped. I hadn't heard Mr Lethman come back, but he was there, with Jassim behind him, coming quickly along the shaded side of the arcade, and looking as if he'd been hurrying. Or, I thought, as if he'd had a slightly dicey interview. At least he looked wide awake now, even brisk.

'She'll see me?'

'Yes, she'll see you, but I'm afraid it'll have to be later tonight.' He made an apologetic gesture. 'I'm sorry, I did try to persuade her, but I told you, it's not a good day, so I didn't like to press it. She's had a touch of bronchial asthma lately, nothing to worry about, but it sometimes prevents her from sleeping. She won't hear of calling the doctor, and since we still had the prescription from last autumn – it was the same trouble then – I didn't overrule her. In a way it's the remedy that's the trouble, rather than the disease. She finds it depressive. To tell you the truth, the idea of a visit from you cheered her up a good deal.'

'That's wonderful. I promise not to tire her.'

'Have you made arrangements with your driver? I'll fix you up with a room now, before I go back to your great-aunt.'

'It's all settled. Hamid's coming back for me tomorrow.'

'Fine,' he said, as if he meant it. 'Well, if you'll come with me, Jassim will show your driver the way back to the gate.'

As I said goodbye to Hamid, I thought I saw Jassim looking at me rather longingly, as if he would have liked to throw me out, too. But he eventually shuffled off into the shadows, and Hamid, with a final cheerful wave to me, went after him.

Mr Lethman led me the other way, towards the rear of the buildings.

'So she didn't take much persuading after all?' I said.

'None at all,' he admitted, 'once she'd grasped who you were. To be honest she couldn't remember much about you, but she's very keen to see you now.'

'I had a feeling she might be. Sheer roaring curiosity, I suppose.'

He glanced down with what looked like surprise. 'Well . . . yes, you could say so. Don't you mind?'

'Why should I? The motive doesn't matter as long as the result's all right. She's seeing me, isn't she? Anyway, it's only fair. What d'you imagine *my* main motive is for visiting Dar Ibrahim?'

'I – yes, of course.' He sounded disconcerted.

'What's the matter? For goodness' sake, does that shock you?'

'No. But . . . you're a very unusual girl, aren't you?'

'Because I insist on my own way, or because I don't think relations are obliged to be fond of one another whether they like it or not? It's not unusual, it's only that most people won't admit it.' I laughed. 'Oh yes, I like to go my own way, but I recognise other people's right to do the same thing. It's about the only thing in my favour.'

'What if their way isn't the same as yours?'

'Oh, if I feel really strongly about anything, it's full steam ahead and damn the torpedoes, but I'm open to argument. Where are you going to put me?'

'In the Seraglio.'

'Well, that's putting me in my place, isn't it? Under lock and key?'

'Just about. At least, all the windows are barred.' He smiled down at me, suddenly charming. 'It's only because it's the best end of the palace, I assure you . . . We may be grudging hosts, but once we've had to give in, we do the thing properly. First-class accommodation, to make up for lack of welcome. Did you know that the Lady Hester Stanhope graded her guests according to status? I believe the third-class used to get a pretty rough night.'

'She would. It's nice of you to top-grade me when I'm giving you all this trouble.'

'Heavens, it's no trouble. Actually I'm delighted you're staying – your great-aunt isn't the only one who likes company . . . I'm simply relieved she took it this way and I didn't have to quarrel with you. I'm certain your visit will do her a world of good – in fact, I can't help thinking it would be nice if she took a sudden shine to you and pressed you to stay for a few weeks, then *you* can sit and read the Koran to her at three in the morning, and give me a night off.'

'Is that what you do?'

'It has been known. Shall I suggest it to her? How long can you spare?'

'I'll let you know in the morning.'

He laughed, and pushed open a wooden gate that hung a bit crooked under a weed-grown arch.

'In here,' he said, and ushered me past him.

4

And still a Garden by the Water blows . . .

                    E. FitzGerald: *The Rubáiyát*
                        of Omar Khayyám

'OH!' I said, and stood still.

John Lethman shut the gate behind him, and came to my elbow. 'Do you like it?'

'*Like* it!' I drew a breath. 'What did it used to be?'

'Oh, just the Seraglio Garden. I'm afraid it's terribly neglected.'

It was, of course, but this was a large part of its beauty. After the prospects of sun-baked stone and dusty ruin that had been assaulting my eyes all afternoon, the riot of green and flowers and the shimmer of cool water was wonderful.

It followed the now familiar pattern of the courtyards, a paved space decorated with flowers and bushes, with a pool at the centre, surrounded by shaded arcades out of which opened the various rooms and offices. But this place was huge. Apparently the Seraglio rooms and garden filled the whole width of the palace, stretching well back over the surface of the plateau. On three sides of this vast space ran the arches of the long colonnades, throwing their pattern of sun and shadow over the doorways of what had been the women's apartments. On the fourth side – to the north – the colonnade marched with the outer wall where a row of delicate arches looked out across the Nahr el-Sal'q towards the village and the distant snows of the High Lebanon. High though these windows were, they were heavily barred with lattices so close that a hand could hardly have been thrust through them.

Within this frame of columns, long ago, some expert had laid out a big formal garden, and had somehow led water down from some high spring to feed the trees and flowers and fill the pool – no ornamental pond this time, but a wide stretch of water, almost a lake, which held at its centre a small island crowned with a grove of trees. On this, at the heart of the green grove, I saw the glint of gilded tiles – the roof of a miniature building like an exotic summerhouse or folly; a Persian-style kiosk with an onion dome, decorative pillars and latticed arches and shallow, broken steps.

There had once been a bridge across to the island, a slender, pretty affair; but now half-way over a broken gap yawned, some six feet wide. The lake itself was paved thickly with lily leaves, and at the edge the irises had spread into dense battalions of spears. All round the brink went a wide paved walk where ferns and briars thrust up the cracked marble slabs. From the shingled roofs of the arcades and down between the pillars jasmine and purple bougainvillaea and roses hung festooned like cobwebs, and every cornice was white with birds' droppings and fully inhabited by doves calling '*Yusuf, Yusuf*', like mad things. The contrast between the formal design of oblong lake, graceful arches and elegant kiosk, and the riotous natural growth that had invaded them, was excitingly attractive. It was like a formal Persian painting gone wild.

'Not a weed out of place,' I said. 'It's gorgeous! And to think I was always sorry for those poor women. Well, that settles it, Mr Lethman, I'll move in tomorrow for a long, long stay. How long can you do with me?'

'Wait till you've seen your room before you commit yourself,' he said, leading the way.

The room was midway along the south side of the garden. It was a plain square room, with a highish ceiling and chequered marble floor and patterned mosaic on the walls in panels of blue and gilt framing texts of Arabic writing. Unlike the other rooms I had seen so far, this one was clean, and well-lighted by a triple window which looked straight out over the Adonis gorge. The window was barred, but not so heavily as those which gave on the plateau. And for obvious reasons: the outer wall of the Seraglio apparently rose straight from the edge of the rock above the river.

'The bedroom's next door,' said Mr Lethman, 'and the bathroom's the one after that. When I say "bathroom", of course, I mean the whole works, a hammam – steam rooms, cold rooms, massage rooms, the lot.' He grinned, 'But guess what, no steam.'

'Any hot?'

'You can't be serious? But there is running water, straight off the snow, and it's all yours.' The smile faded, and he looked at me a little doubtfully. 'You know, it's terribly brave of you to stay. We're not geared for this kind of thing.'

'I'm enjoying it,' I said truthfully.

'I suppose whatever else it is, this end of the place must seem like a slice of real Eastern romance? Heaven knows I hope you can keep your illusions . . . I'm afraid the bedroom's not ready yet. I'll send Halide along to fix it up in a minute, and bring you some towels. Is there anything else you'll want?'

'Only a toothbrush, and I don't suppose the hammam runs to that. Don't look so worried, I was only joking. I'll do very well for one night, if supper could possibly include an apple? I hope Great-Aunt Harriet's régime does run to supper?'

He laughed. 'Have a heart. What's more, you'll be glad to hear that Halide doesn't feed me on your great-aunt's diet! I'll have to leave you now, I'm afraid.' He glanced at his watch. 'You'd like a drink, I'm sure. I'll send one straight away. It'll soon be too dark for you to explore much, but go where you like – except for the Prince's rooms, of course, and either Halide or I will be there to fend you off if you lose your way.'

'Thanks, but I'll just stay here. The garden's lovely.'

'Then I'll be back to join you in about half an hour, and we'll eat.'

When he had gone I sat down on the divan cushions, looking out over the gorge where the last of the light netted the tips of the trees with gold. Below, the shadows deepended through purple to black. It would soon be dark. I realised suddenly that I was tired, and hoped that when Halide came with the drink it wouldn't be the conventional Arab welcome of arak.

It wasn't, and it wasn't brought by Halide, but by a stocky young Arab who was presumably the brother, Nasirulla. He was dressed like Jassim in white robes, and came in silently with a tray which held a lighted lamp, two glasses, and a bottle of the golden wine of the Bk'aa. This is a lovely wine, light and dryish and about the best that Lebanon produces, and he couldn't have brought anything I'd sooner have had at that moment. I began to think kindly of Mr John Lethman.

When I spoke to Nasirulla he eyed me sidelong, shook his head, and said something in Arabic. Then he set the lamp in a niche near the door, sketched a salaam, and went out.

With the coming of the lamp the darkness, as it always does, seemed to fall quickly. Only minutes after Nasirulla had left me the blue sky beyond the windows dimmed to blackness, and by seven o'clock it was quite dark.

I sat curled on the window-seat, sipping the golden wine, and wondering what the night would bring.

It was very quiet. The night sky was like black velvet spangled with big stars, and, as if it had indeed been a velvet curtain, all sound seemed to be cut off, even the faintest murmuring of the river below my window. In the garden the doves had fallen silent and not even a breath of air stirred the feathery trees. Through the open door I could smell jasmine and roses, and some other strongly scented flowers, and below those exotic scents, as a sort of reminding undertone, the sweetish stagnant smell of the pool.

Mr Lethman came back at about a quarter to eight, and with him Nasirulla with the supper tray. There was soup, scalding hot in a big Thermos jug, and a dish of *shawarma* – mutton flavoured with vinegar, lemon, onion and cardamom seeds and grilled on a long spit. With this came a bowl of salad, a dish of pale butter and half a goats' milk cheese, a pile of unleavened bread and some apples and another bottle of wine. Nasirulla put this down on the low table, said something to Mr Lethman, and then left us.

I said: 'If you call this living simply, count me in.'

He laughed. 'I told you Halide fed me extra on the side. By the way, Nasirulla says she's on her way to do your room now.'

'I'm giving you a lot of trouble. I mean, bringing the tray all this way for one thing. Where d'you usually eat?'

'Here, quite often.' He added apologetically: 'You'll probably find out, so I may as well tell you, these are my rooms. No, listen, please . . . I was going to sleep over the other side tonight anyway, so you're not to think you've put us to any trouble at all.'

'Not put you to—? Mr Lethman, I don't know what to say! Turning you out of your room!'

But he cut short my protestations by serving the soup and handing me mine in an eared round mug along with some Arab bread, then refilling my wineglass. It seemed almost as if he were bent on making amends for his earlier reluctance to let me in; or as if, once the Lady Harriet had accepted me, traditional Arab hospitality must have its way, and there was literally not enough that he and the Arab servants could do to make my stay a comfortable one. Any connection between my lively host and the harassed, sleep- or smoke-bemused young man of the afternoon seemed purely coincidental. He seemed to be laying himself out to entertain me, and we chatted pleasantly throughout the meal.

He knew a fair amount about the history of the place, and was very entertaining about what he called the Lady's 'cut-price court' of Dar Ibrahim, but I noticed that he said very little about Great-Aunt Harriet herself, and behind his reserve I thought I could sense respect and liking for her. Whatever else he mocked, and however much she might invite it, he did not mock his patroness, and I liked him the better for it. He was certainly interested in everything I could tell him about the family. The only thing I refrained deliberately from mentioning was Charles's presence in Syria, and the fact that he, too, was planning a visit. I intended to find a good moment to tell Great-Aunt Harriet myself that he wanted to see her, and so by-pass all the difficulties of persuasion at second-hand. Not that, if Charles was right, any persuasion would be needed. If she had agreed so readily to see me, whom she would hardly remember, then her favourite Charles was practically in already.

Halide brought coffee at nine o'clock, with the

information that Nasirulla had gone back to the village, and that my room was ready.

She was not much like her brother in appearance, being younger and slimly built. She was a dark-skinned Arab, walnut rather than olive, with huge dark eyes, slim neck and delicate hands. Her dress was of bronze-green silk, a rich-looking material and a sophisticated colour; her eyes were outlined with black in a way London would have recognised; and under the thin silk she wore, unless I was mistaken, a French – a very French – half-cup bra. Like a great many Arab women she wore her bank account on her wrists, which jingled with thin gold bracelets. No simple Arab maiden this one, and – if I was any judge – wasting no sweetness on the desert air. As she told Mr Lethman (in English) about the room, she looked me over in her turn, and the message passed, clear from female to female in any language from Eskimo to Aborigine: 'Not that he'd look at you, the mess you look in those trousers, but keep off my patch, will you, or I'll make you sorry.'

Then, with the black eyes modestly lowered, she was saying to John Lethman, in her pretty, softly-accented English: 'When you have finished your coffee, the Lady would like to see you again.'

She went out, leaving the door open. I watched her slim graceful figure vanish into the shadows of the arcade, beyond the small light cast by the lamp; but I thought she hadn't gone very far. In a moment or two I knew that I was right: where the waters of the lake reflected a faint greyness from the star-filled sky I saw a movement. She was waiting among the bushes by the water's edge, probably watching us through the open door.

John Lethman made no move to shut it. Since he was obviously anxious to finish his coffee and answer the summons, I hurried with mine, too.

Soon he got to his feet. 'I'm afraid I'll have to leave you now, but I'll come back as soon as she lets me, and take you across. Now, are you sure you'll be all right here?'

'Why not? Don't worry about me, I'll be fine. I'll find a book.'

'Of course, take anything you want. You can turn the lamp up quite easily if it's not bright enough; Halide'll show you how.'

He turned his head sharply as a bell jangled somewhere deep in the buildings, sounding very loud in the hushed night. And from somewhere nearer, startled off by the violent and prolonged pealing of the bell, came the sudden furious baying of dogs. Big dogs, by the sound of them, inside the building, and quite near.

'What on earth's happened?' I demanded, startled.

'Just your great-aunt getting impatient. I'll have to go, I'm sorry. I'll be back to fetch you as soon as I can.'

'But those dogs?'

'Oh, that's nothing, they always make that hellish noise when the bell goes. Don't worry about them, I'll shut them up before I come back for you.'

' "Shut them up?" You mean they're loose about the place? They sound dangerous.'

'Well, they're our watchdogs, they have to be. But they're only turned loose at night, and they can't get into the Seraglio if you keep the main door shut. You'll be quite safe.' He flashed me a sudden smile. 'Not to worry, it's not your night for being eaten alive – at least, not by the dogs.'

He went. I heard the wooden gate shut behind him, and a few moments later his voice calling to the dogs. The baying stopped, and silence came back. In it I saw Halide, glimmering in the doorway in her green silk.

'If you will come this way, I will show you your room.'

She had lit another lamp for me in the bedroom, and set it on a shelf near the bed.

This room was a twin of the other, but seemed bigger, as it contained no furniture but a narrow iron-framed bed, a flimsy-looking bamboo chair, and a hideous chest of drawers painted black, which held a rather beautiful lacquered looking-glass and a battered old tin box with metal clasps labelled S.S. *Yangtse Maid*. The floor was bare and so were the window-seats on the dais. The bed was made up with Irish linen, yellowish and not very well ironed, and the red honeycomb quilt covered what looked like the hardest and healthiest mattress in the world.

I didn't think somehow that this was Halide's patch; there would have to be a good deal more Eastern glamour about any affairs of hers. Was that what John Lethman had meant by 'sleeping on the other side'?

However, it wasn't this thought which made me say: 'I've turned Mr Lethman out, haven't I? Where will he sleep?'

A shrug, not quite insolent. 'There are plenty of

rooms.' When I didn't answer she glanced at me, perhaps a bit uneasily, and added with an attempt at civility dragged up with obvious difficulty: 'He is with the Lady often at night. He'll maybe sleep in the morning.'

'Oh, well, perhaps I haven't upset things as much as I thought.' I smiled at her. 'But I'm afraid it's giving you a lot of trouble, changing the rooms round twice.'

She didn't make the usual disclaimer, but this may only have been because her English wasn't good enough for polite skirmishing.

'You have seen the bathroom?'

'Yes, thanks. Is the water drinkable?'

'Yes, but there was water on the supper tray. I will leave that. If there is nothing else—?'

'I don't think so, thank you. It all looks very nice, and I'm sure I shall be comfortable. Oh, would you show me how to turn the lamp higher, please? Mr Lethman said I might look at his books while I was waiting.'

Back in the other room she obliged, lifting the lamp down and setting it on the table among the books. I thanked her, and examined them while she began to stack the used dishes on the tray. She said nothing more, but I saw how she watched me, and it wasn't imagination to read a wary hostility into those quick sidelong glances. Irritated now, and wishing she would finish her job and go. I concentrated on selecting a book. As light reading for whiling away an hour or two they were hardly promising. An Arabic grammar, a few books on Syria and the Lebanon which I had already read during my convalescence in Charles's room, and a collection which might be said to represent John Lethman's homework – some volumes (also familiar to me) about the original Lady of the Lebanon: Joan Haslip and Roundell and Silk Buckingham and the three old volumes of Dr Meryon's diary about his redoubtable patroness. I looked at the fly-leaves. As I thought, they were Great-Aunt Harriet's own copies, presumably lent to her latter-day 'Dr Meryon' for his close study . . . I skipped along the row. T. E. Lawrence's *Crusader Castles*, Guillaume's *Islam*, the Everyman *Koran*, King-lake's *Eothen* . . . all Aunt Harriet's. No medical textbooks, which were presumably too bulky to carry on field work. The only things which carried his own name were – interestingly enough – Huxley's *The Mind Changers*, Fraser's *Golden Bough*, and a newish paper-bound copy of Théophile Gautier's *Le Club des Hachachiens*. No novels except Dostoevsky's *The Brothers Karamazov* and Margery Allingham's *The Tiger in the Smoke*.

The last volume in the row was de Quincey. I turned the pages idly while Halide stacked the dishes rather loudly on the tray.

'The opium-eater loses none of his moral sensibilities, or aspirations: he wishes and longs, as earnestly as ever, to realise what he believes possible, and feels to be exacted by duty; but his intellectual apprehension of what is possible infinitely out-runs his power, not of execution only, but even of power to attempt. He lies under the weight of incubus and nightmare . . .'

Plus ça change, plus c'est la même chose. It was exactly what Hamid had said. I put the opium nightmare back as Halide lifted the tray and went with it to the door.

'I'll shut it for you,' I said, moving to do so, but she paused in the doorway and turned.

'You are really the daughter of the Lady's brother's son?'

I worked it out while she stared at me across the dishes.

'Yes.'

'Your father is also here in the Lebanon?'

'No.'

'He is dead?'

'No,' I said, surprised. 'Why?'

'Then you travel alone?'

'Why not?'

She ignored this, too. She was intent on some line of her own which I couldn't follow, but which was obviously intensely important to her.

'You – you stay here long?'

Curiosity made me less than truthful. 'As long as she'll let me,' I said, watching her.

She said quickly: 'She is not well. You will have to go in the morning.'

I raised my brows. 'That's for her to say, surely?' I added, with innocence concealing a flicker of malice: 'But of course in a place this size I needn't be in her way. Mr Lethman asked me to stay as long as I liked.'

The black eyes flared, whether in alarm or anger it was impossible to say. 'But that is not possible! He—'

Jangling, imperative, and sounding very bad-tempered, Great-Aunt Harriet's bell shattered the silence once more. Farther away, but still obviously at large, the watchdogs bayed. The girl started, so violently that the things on the tray clashed and rattled.

'Saved by the bell,' I said. 'You were saying?'

'No. No. I must go!' Then, almost fiercely, as I made a move to follow and open the main gate for her: 'Leave it! I can manage, I can manage!'

The gate shut behind her. I stared thoughtfully after her. Saved by the bell, indeed. I thought I could add the score. Whether or not John Lethman had a stake in Great-Aunt Harriet, I was sure that Halide had a stake in John Lethman. And I wasn't sure how that added up for Great-Aunt Harriet. I went back to the bookshelf.

It would be nice to be able to record that I was the kind of person who would pick up the Dostoevsky or the Huxley or even *The Golden Bough* and curl up with it for a glorious evening's read. But when eventually Mr Lethman came for me as he had promised, he found me a few chapters into *The Tiger in the Smoke*, and half-wishing I had chosen something less exciting for a night in the deserted wing of a ruined palace.

He was armed, not with an oil lamp, but with an enormous and very powerful electric torch.

'Ready?' he asked.

He led me back to the courtyard where Hamid and I had waited, but there we turned right, away from the main gate, the way I had seen him go to Great-Aunt Harriet. The place was vast, far bigger even than I had imagined. We seemed to walk for ever up corridors, round corners, up steps, down steps, and across at least two more small courts, in the first of which a trickle of water showed that all the wells had not dried. As we traversed the second I heard, from behind a closed door, a scratching sound followed by a deep whining yelp that made me jump.

'It's all right, I told you I'd shut them up.' He shone the torch momentarily towards the door, and in the gap at its foot I saw the gleam of a dog's damp nose snuffing at the air. 'Sofi! Star! Quiet there! Watch your step, Miss Mansel, the threshold's broken here. This is the Prince's Garden.'

I don't know quite what I had expected, something at least as grand as the Seraglio Garden, but in fact the Prince's Garden was very small. The air was heavy with the scent of jasmine, and I caught a glimpse in the torchlight of a low wall which might contain a pool, but the garden seemed to be little more than an oblong yard with one or two troughs of flowers and some small symmetrical trees in tubs. John Lethman shone the torch straight down on the cracked slabs of the foot-way, but he could have saved himself the trouble, for, from an open doorway about half-way along the side of the garden, light was spilling out between two small tubbed trees. It was only the dim orange light from a lamp like the one in my own room, but in the heavy darkness it seemed very bright.

He paused in the doorway to stand aside for me. His voice sounded different all at once, tight, wary, defer-ential.

'I've brought Miss Mansel, Lady Harriet.'

I went past him into the room.

5

There came
A tongue of light, a fit of flame;
And Christable saw the lady's eye,
And nothing else saw she thereby . . .
S. T. Coleridge: *Christabel*

THE Prince's Divan was enormous, and in it prevailed what I can only call a luxurious squalor. The floor was of coloured marble, strewn here and there with Persian rugs, all very dirty; the walls were patterned with intricate mosaics, each panel framing in fretted stone a recess which must once have held a statue or lamp, but which was now empty except for an accumulation of rubbish – cartons, papers, books, medicine bottles, candle-stubs. In the centre of the floor the fountain had been roughly boarded over and now did duty as a table where stood a large tray of greyish silver holding a pile of plates and the remains of a recent meal. Beside this, on the floor, was an empty bowl labelled DOG. A chest of drawers in shiny mahogany, covered with more bottles and pill-boxes, stood against the wall. One or two shabby kitchen chairs and a big throne-like affair in red Chinese lacquer completed the furniture of the lower end of the room. Dust lay everywhere.

A wide archway of delicately chiselled stone framing three shallow steps divided the lower from the upper section of the divan. Set right back in one corner of the upper room or dais was a huge bed, which at one time must have been a luxurious affair with legs shaped like dragons' claws, a high carved head-board, and hanging from the ceiling above it some sort of gilt device resembling a bird, which was supposed to have held bed-drapes in its talons, Now one wing of the bird was broken, the gilt was flaked and dirty, and from the claws hung only a couple of rubbed velvet curtains which could have been any shade from dark red to black, and which sagged in big loops down on either side of the bed-head, almost concealing with their heavy swags of shadow the figure which reclined in a welter of rugs and blankets.

The light which had flowed so generously out on the flag-way of the garden hardly penetrated into the upper corners of the room. It came from an old-fashioned oil lamp standing among the supper dishes, and as I passed it, approaching the bed, my shadow seemed to leap monstrously ahead of me, then teeter up the steps of the dais to add another layer of darkness to the grotesque obscurity in the corner.

For grotesque it certainly was. I had expected to find Great-Aunt Harriet very different from a child's far-back recollections of her, but not quite so outlandish as this. As I had told John Lethman, I had retained merely a dim memory of a tallish hook-nosed woman with

greying hair and snapping black eyes who argued
fiercely with my father, bullied my mother over the
garden, and had a habit of bestowing sudden and
exotic gifts on me and Charles, in the intervals of
ignoring us completely. Even had she been dressed
as she was fifteen years before, I should not have
known her. John Lethman had warned me that she
would have shrunk, and this was so; and though I
thought I would have recognised the jutting nose and
black eyes which peered at me from the shadows of the
bed curtains, nothing – not even Lethman's warnings –
had prepared me for the sheer outlandishness of the
figure which sat there like a Buddha cocooned in
coloured silks and gesturing with one large pale hand
for me to come nearer.

If I had not known who it was, I should have taken
her for some fantastically-robed Eastern male. She was
wearing some kind of bedgown of natural silk, and over
this a loose coat in scarlet velvet with gold facings, and
over this again an enormous cashmere shawl; but these
draperies – in spite of the soft and even luxurious
materials – had a distinctly masculine air. Her skin had
a sallow pallor and her lips were bloodless and sunken,
but the black eyes and well-marked brows gave life to
the fullish, oval face, and showed none of the fading
signs of old age. She had daubed powder lavishly and
carelessly, and some of it had spilled over the scarlet
velvet. Above this curiously epicene face she had
twined a towering turban of white, which, slipping a
little to one side, exposed what for a shocked moment I
took to be a bald skull; then I realised she must have

shaved her head. This, if she habitually wore a thick turban, was only to be expected, but it was somehow the final touch of grotesqueness.

One thing I would have known her by; the ring on her left hand. This was unequivocally as big and as bright as I remembered from my childhood. I remembered, too, how impressed Charles and I had been by the way my mother and father spoke of the ring. It was a cabochon-cut Burma ruby, the size of a thumb-nail, and had even in those days been immensely valuable. It had been the gift of some princeling in Baghdad, and she wore it always on her big, capable and rather mannish hands. The ruby flashed in the lamplight as, wheezing a little, she beckoned me closer.

I didn't know whether I would be expected to kiss her. The idea was somehow repellent, but another glitter from the ruby, indicating a stool near the foot of the bed, halted me thankfully.

'Hullo, Aunt Harriet, how are you?'

'Well, Christy?' The voice, little more than a whisper, had a strained, asthmatic breathiness, but the black eyes were live enough, and curious. 'Sit down and let me look at you. Hm. Yes. You always were a pretty little thing. Quite a beauty now, aren't you? Not married yet?'

'No.'

'Then it's high time you were.'

'Have a heart, I'm only twenty-two!'

'Is that all? One forgets. John tells me I forget things all the time. I'd forgotten you, did he tell you that?'

'He said it was quite likely.'

'He would. He's always trying to make out that I'm getting senile.' She darted a look at John Lethman, who had followed me up the steps and was standing at the foot of the bed. He watched her steadily, and I thought uneasily. The sharp gaze came back to me. 'And if I did forget you, it'd be hardly surprising. How long since I saw you?'

'Fifteen years.'

'Hm. Yes. It must be. Well, now I come to look at you I suppose I would have known you. You've a look of your father. How is he?'

'Oh, he's fine, thank you.'

'Sends his dear love, I suppose?'

The tone, still sharp, was wantonly provocative. I regarded her calmly.

'If he knew I was here, I'm sure he'd send his regards.'

'Hm.' She sat back abruptly in her corner against the pile of pillows; retreating into her cocoon of draperies with the little settling motions of a broody hen spreading herself down on to eggs. I thought the monosyllable was not unappreciative. 'And the rest of 'em?'

'All well. They'll be terribly pleased when they hear I've managed to see you, and found you well.'

'No doubt.' No one could have called the dry whisper senile. 'An attentive family the Mansels, wouldn't you say? Well?' And again when I didn't speak: 'Well, girl?'

I sat up straight on my stool. It was very uncomfortable. 'I don't know what you want me to say, Aunt Harriet. If you think we should have come to see you before, you could always have asked us, couldn't you? As it is, you know quite well you've been sending us all to the devil, solo and chorus, about twice a year for fifteen years. And if you'll forgive my saying so, I wasn't exactly welcomed with open arms today!' I added crisply: 'In any case, you're a Mansel, too. You can't tell me my people don't write to you just as often as you write to them, even if it's only to thank you for the latest edition of your Will!'

The black eyes glittered. 'My Will? Ha! So that's it! Come to collect, have you?'

'Well, I'd have a job, since you're still alive, wouldn't I?' I grinned at her. 'And it's a heck of a long way to come for six-pence . . . But if you like you can give me my sixpence here and now, and I won't bother you again.'

I couldn't see her expression, just the eyes, shadowed under brows and turban, watching me from the pillows. I caught a glance from John Lethman, half amused, I thought, and half apprehensive, as she stirred suddenly, plucking at the coverings. 'I could have died out here for all they'd have cared. Any of them.'

'Look—' I said, then stopped. Charles had implied that she liked to be outfaced, and certainly up to now I had had the impression that she was trying to needle me. But the Great-Aunt Harriet that I had remembered wouldn't have talked like that, not even to provoke a retort. Fifteen years seems a lifetime to the young: perhaps at the other end it's a lifetime, too. I ought to be feeling, not discomfort and irritation, but compassion.

I said quickly: 'Aunt Harriet, look, please don't talk
like that! You must know quite well that if there was
anything you wanted – anything you needed – you've
only got to let Daddy know, or Uncle Chas, or any of
us! My family's been in America for four years, you
know that, and I suppose we're a bit out of touch, but
in any case it was always Uncle Chas you wrote to, and
I understood from him – I mean, I thought you'd
always made it so very clear that you wanted to stay
out here, live on your own terms . . .' I made a vague,
wide gesture that took in the neglected room and
beyond it the dark confines of the sleeping palace.
'You must surely know that if there was anything – if
you were ill – if you really did want someone to come
here, or needed help of some kind—'

Deep in its shadowed corner the bundle on the bed
was so still that I faltered. The lamp had been burning
low, but now some trick of the draught or unevenness
of the wick sent up a tongue of light, and I saw the
quick glitter of her eyes. It wasn't pathos at all. The
instinct that was forbidding me to feel compassion had
been right.

'Aunt H!' I said roundly. 'Are you sending me up? I
mean, you're just teasing, aren't you? You must know
you're talking nonsense!'

'Hm. Nonsense, is it? Meaning that I have got a
devoted family?'

'Well, heavens, you know what families are! I don't
suppose ours is any different from any other! You must
know quite well you could cut us all off with sixpence
till you're blue in the face, but we're still your family!'

'Hear that, John?'

He was looking, I thought, acutely uncomfortable. He opened his mouth to say something, but I cut across it:

'You know quite well what I mean! Just that if you needed anything, or anything happened to you – well, London to Beirut only takes six hours, and someone would be here and raising the place before you even knew you wanted them. Daddy always says that's what a family is, it's just collective insurance; as long as you're alive and well it just goes ticking along and takes no notice, but let anything go wrong, and the company moves in. Heavens, I do what I like, and nobody stops me going where I want to, but I know quite well that if I was in the least spot of trouble and got on the phone to Daddy, he'd be here in three seconds!' I looked up at John Lethman, hesitated, then added decisively: 'And don't start teasing Mr Lethman as well. It doesn't matter what you say to me, but I might as well make something else clear here and now, even if I may be speaking out of turn . . . Everybody'll be as pleased as Punch that he's here with you, so you'd better be nice to him, because the longer he stays the better! For goodness' sake, we're not neglecting you – we're just letting you get on with it the way you want to, and you seem to be making a pretty good job of it, if you ask me!'

She was laughing openly now, the cocoon heaving to the wheezing breaths. The big hand went up, and the ruby flashed. 'All right, child, all right, I was teasing you! A fighter, aren't you? I always did like a fighter.

No, I don't make it easy for people to get in to see me;
I've had too much trouble that way, and say what you
like, I'm getting old. You were very insistent, weren't
you? If you're so full of this "live and let live" of yours,
why did you come?'

I grinned. 'You'd be annoyed if I said it was family
feeling. Call it curiosity.'

'What had you heard to make you so curious?'

'What had I heard? You must be joking! I suppose
you're so used to living in a place like this and hedging
yourself with legends like a – well, like a—'

'Superannuated Sleeping Beauty?'

I laughed. 'Bang on! I mean, yes, if you like to put it
that way! But seriously, you're a celebrity, you knew
that! Everybody talks about you. You're one of the
sights of the Lebanon. Even if I'd been no relation I'd
have been told all about you and urged to come and
look at Dar Ibrahim; so when I realised I had a copper-
bottomed excuse to call to see you, and even bull-doze
my way into the palace – well, boiling oil might have
stopped me, but nothing short of that.'

'Make a note of that, John; boiling oil is what we
need. Hm, you're a Mansel to your claw-tips, aren't
you? So everybody talks about me, do they? Who's
"everybody"?'

'Oh, this was just someone in the hotel in Beirut. I
was planning a trip—'

'Hotel? Who were you chattering about me to in a
hotel in Beirut?' She made it sound as if it were a
brothel in Cairo.

'Not exactly chattering. It was the desk clerk, as it

happens. I was planning a trip up to the Adonis Source at Afka, and he told me I'd be passing near Dar Ibrahim, and—'

'Which hotel?'

'The Phoenicia.'

'It's new since you were in Beirut,' put in John Lethman. It was the first time he had spoken. He still seemed ill at ease. 'It's the big one I told you about, on the harbour.'

'The what? Phoenicia? All right, go on, what were they saying about me in this hotel?'

'Nothing much, really,' I said. 'The desk clerk didn't know I was a relation of yours, he was just telling me this was an interesting place, and he said I might as well get my driver to come back by Sal'q and stop so that I could get a view of the palace. Then I told him I knew your family – I still didn't tell him who I was – and asked how you were and if he'd heard anything about you.'

'And what did he tell you?'

'Only that as far as he knew you were perfectly all right, but that you hadn't been outside the palace for quite a time, and he told me you'd been ill a short while back, and had a doctor from Beirut—'

'He knew that?'

'Well, heavens, it was probably in all the papers! You're one of the local legends, after all! Didn't Mr Lethman tell you, I rang the doctor's house up to try to get news of you—'

'Yes, yes, yes, he told me. A lot of use that would have been. The man was a fool. A good thing he's gone, a very good thing . . . Much better now, much better.' The shawl had slipped; she pulled at it with a sort of flouncing irritation, suddenly pettish, and I heard her muttering to herself what sounded like 'Ringing up about me,' and 'Chattering about me in hotels,' in a whisper which was all at once not dry and sharp at all, but vague and blurred. Her head shook, so that the turban was dislodged even further, exposing a little more of that shaved scalp.

I looked away, repelled, and trying not to show it. But wherever I looked was a reminder of a slovenly eccentricity; even the clutter of medicine bottles on the chest was dusty, and dust gritted under my shoes as I shifted my feet on the floor. The room, big as it was, felt stuffy, and my skin prickled. I found myself suddenly longing to escape into fresh air.

'Christy . . . Christy . . .' The wheezing mutter jerked my attention back to her. 'Stupid name for a girl, What's it short for?'

'Christabel. It was the nearest they could get to Christopher.'

'Oh.' She plucked at the covers again. I got the sharp impression that the eyes watching me from the shadows were by no means forgetful; that this was a game she played when it suited her. The impression wasn't pleasant. 'What were we talking about?'

I pulled myself together. 'The doctor. Dr Grafton.'

'I was not ill; the man was a fool. There's nothing wrong with my chest, nothing at all . . . In any case, he's left the Lebanon. Wasn't there some chatter about him, too, John? Some scandal? Didn't he go back to London?'

'I believe so,' said Lethman.

I said: 'They told me so when I rang up. They didn't say anything else about him.'

'Hm,' she said, and all the dry malice was back in her voice. 'Probably put his plate up in Wimpole Street by now and making a fortune.'

'I never heard any scandal, but it's true he's gone. They say his practice went to a very good man.' John Lethman gave me a quick, speaking look, and then leaned forward. 'Now don't you think you should have a rest, Lady Harriet? It's time for your tablets, so if you'll allow me, I'll ring for Halide, and see Miss Mansel back myself—'

'No,' said Great-Aunt Harriet uncompromisingly.

'But, Lady Harriet—'

'I tell you, boy, stop fussing. I won't take the tablets yet, they make me sleepy. You know I don't like taking them. I'm not tired at all, and I'm enjoying the gel's visit. Stay where you are, child, and talk to me. Entertain me. Tell me where you've been and what you've been doing. How long have you been in Beirut?'

'Only since Friday evening. Actually, I came with a package tour . . .'

I started to tell her about the trip, making it as amusing as I could. I wouldn't be sorry when the interview was over, but the old lady seemed back on the beam now, and I had no intention of letting John Lethman, on whatever excuse, winkle me out of the presence chamber until I had, so to speak, introduced

Charles. He wouldn't want to miss this bizarre set-up, and he wouldn't be likely to be put off by what I had to tell him. I wondered in passing why she hadn't spoken of him herself, but I would soon discover that, and it was up to my cousin to fight his own way in past the opposition if he wished to.

So I kept clear of his name, and talked away about Petra and Palmyra and Jerash, while Great-Aunt Harriet listened and commented, apparently well entertained, and John Lethman waited in silence, fidgeting nervily with the bed-curtains, and with his head turning from one to the other of us like someone at a Wimbledon final.

I was in the middle of describing Palmyra when she startled me suddenly by reaching out a hand and yanking at a bell-pull which hung among the curtains of the bed. The building echoed to the familiar clanging peal, and then to the noise of the baying hounds.

I stopped talking, but she said almost snappily: 'Go on. At least you can talk. Did you visit the hillside tombs?'

'Heavens, yes, there was a conducted tour, we had to: I suppose that's not the right thing to say to an archaeologist, but one tomb looks very like another to me, I'm afraid.'

'True enough. What happened to the party?'

'They went back to London on Saturday morning.'

'So you're on your own now? Is that suitable?'

I laughed. 'Why not? I can look after myself. And as a matter of fact—'

'Not much doubt of that. Where's that stupid girl?'

She snapped it suddenly at John Lethman, who jumped. 'Halide? She can't be far away. If it's your pills, I can—'

'Not my pills. I told you I'll not take them yet. I want my pipe.'

'But, Lady Harriet—'

'Ah, there you are! Where the devil were you?'

Halide came quickly across the lower part of the room. She could not have been far away when the bell rang, but she breathed fast and shallow as if she had been running. Her face was sallow, and she looked scared. She didn't spare me a glance as she crossed the floor and mounted the steps towards the bed.

'You rang?'

'Of course I rang,' said Great-Aunt Harriet irritably. 'I want my pipe.'

Halide looked uncertainly from her to John Lethman and back again, and the old woman made one of these flouncing impatient movements in the bed and barked: 'Well? Well?'

'Get it for her, please,' said Lethman.

The girl threw another scared glance at the bed, and scurried down the steps to the dressing-chest. I looked after her with a touch of surprise. Nothing so far had led me to think that she would be easily frightened, and it wasn't easy to see how my great-aunt could frighten her, short of the methods used by Lady Hester Stanhope, who kept a whip and club by her bed to use on her slaves, and who when service was poor had treated them all – her doctor included – to a purge she called the Black Draught, forcibly administered. I looked at

the 'Lady Harriet'. She was sitting hunched like some
peculiar Eastern jinnee in her welter of silks and
blankets, and might, I thought, inspire nervousness,
but not fear. But then something caught my eye on the
wall above the bed. There were two sets of pegs in the
wall, half hidden by the bed curtains, and across one of
these lay a stick, and across the other a rifle. I blinked at
these in disbelief. There were surely, in the mid-
twentieth century, limits to what could be done even
here . . . ?

I really must get out of here soon. I must be more
tired than I had thought. Or perhaps the strange food
at supper . . . ? As I pulled myself together to go on
with my story, I heard Great-Aunt Harriet saying,
perfectly pleasantly: 'Just a small pipe, my dear.
And I'll have the amber mouthpiece.'

The girl, hurrying with clumsy fingers, pulled open
a drawer and took out a wooden box which appeared
to hold tobacco and mouthpiece. These she brought
to the bed, and fitted the mouthpiece to the tube of
the apparatus that the Arabs called the *nargileh*, or
hubble-bubble pipe. As she passed out of Great-Aunt
Harriet's view behind the bed-curtains I saw her
throw a quick inquiring glance at John Lethman,
and receive a rather irritable nod. This, then, was
the cause of her nervousness; she was in the familiar,
awkward position of the servant being bidden by one
master to do what she knew the other would dis-
approve.

Lethman said in my ear: 'I can't offer you a cigarette,
I'm afraid, she won't allow anyone else to smoke in

here. In any case she only approves of herbal tobacco. I'm afraid it smells vile.'

'It doesn't matter, I don't want one.'

'What are you muttering about?' asked Great-Aunt Harriet sharply, peering. 'All right, Halide, it's going very well.' Then, to me: 'Well, go on, entertain me. What did you do in Damascus? Tramped round the Great Mosque, I suppose, like a lot of gapeseeds.'

'Exactly like gapeseeds, Aunt Harriet.'

'Are you laughing at me, gel?'

'Well, it's such a gorgeous word. What are they?'

'God knows. Probably aren't any anymore. The world isn't what it used to be.' She sucked at the pipe. 'Did you like Damascus?'

'So-so. I didn't have enough time to myself. But something rather nice happened there, I ran into Charles.'

'Charles?' Her voice was sharp, and I thought I saw Halide and John Lethman look at one another again, quickly. 'Here?' asked Great-Aunt Harriet. 'What's this, a family convention? What the devil's my nephew Charles doing in Damascus?'

'Oh, not Uncle Chas,' I said quickly, 'I meant Charles, my cousin – my "twin". He's on holiday over here, too. He was to have come up with me to see you, but he probably won't be in Lebanon till tomorrow, and I'm afraid I stole a march on him. As a matter of fact it was he who sent me to see you in the first place; he's terribly keen to come himself, and I'd probably never have dared to barge in like this if he hadn't put me up to it.'

There was silence. The pipe bubbled, rather sick-eningly, and she blinked at me through the smoke. The air was acrid, and stuffier than ever, and I felt waves of heat coursing over my skin. I pulled myself upright on my stool.

'You – you do remember Charles, Aunt Harriet? You'll not have forgotten him even if you *had* forgotten me – he was always your favourite.'

'Of course I haven't forgotten him. How could I? A handsome boy. I always liked handsome boys.'

I smiled. 'I used to be jealous, let me tell you! D'you remember that time – the last time I saw you – when you came to stay, and you brought the parrot and all the dogs, and you gave me an ivory fan, and you gave Charles the incense burner and the joss-sticks, and he set the summer-house on fire, and Daddy was so furious he said he was going to send him home, only you said if he went you'd go too because the rest of the family were as dull as ditchwater, and anything Charles did shone like a bad deed in an insipid world? I only remember that because it's a sort of family quotation now.'

'Yes, I remember. The way time goes. Sometimes fast, sometimes slow . . . and the things one remembers . . . and the things one forgets. A handsome boy . . . yes, yes.' She smoked for a while in silence, nodding as if to herself, then relinquished the mouthpiece of the pipe to Halide without looking at her. The black eyes lifted again and fixed on me. 'You're like him.'

'I suppose I am. Not really any more, now we're both grown up . . . though I suppose you remember him fairly recently. Something must persist. We've the same colouring.'

'Very like him.' It was as if she hadn't heard me. She was still nodding to herself, the black eyes veiled and absent, her hands unsteady with her shawl.

'Lady Harriet,' said John Lethman, abruptly. 'I really must insist you take your tablets now, and rest for a little. Miss Mansel—'

'Of course,' I said, getting to my feet, 'if Great-Aunt Harriet will tell me what I'm to say to Charles?'

'You may give him my regards.' The whisper was harsh as the rustle of dry leaves.

'But—' I regarded her a little blankly. 'Don't you want to see him? He'll be in Beirut at the Phoenicia with me, probably tomorrow. May he come up to see you on Monday? Or if it'd be less bother, he could come up tomorrow evening after dinner and wait till you're ready to receive him? He has his own car; he wouldn't need to stay, like me. I'd love to come with him myself and see you again, but if two people are too many—'

'No.'

'You mean we can both come? Oh, that's marvellous! Then—'

'I mean I won't receive him. No, I have received you, and it's been a pleasure, but this is enough. You may take what news you have of me to my nephews Charles and Christopher, and be satisfied with that.'

As I opened my mouth she lifted her hand and added, more kindly: 'All this must be strange to you, but I'm an old woman and I have chosen my way of life, and it seems to me that the only good thing that age brings is the right to be as arbitrary as one wants, and to live as one wishes as long as one can afford it. However outlandish and uncomfortable you may think it is here, it suits me, and you can tell them at home that I'm perfectly well, and quite content with my way of life and the privacy I bought when I bought these high walls and that dumb fool at the gate and what service Halide chooses to offer. So we'll have no more protestations.'

'But he'll be desperately disappointed! And what's more, he'll be furious with me because I've taken his turn with you, so to speak. You were rather his favourite relative, you know. And as a matter of fact, I think it was rather important for him to see you. I don't know whether you knew, but there's a plan under way for opening a branch of the bank in Beirut, and Charles'll probably work there – at least for a time – so while he's out here now I know he wants to make all the contacts—'

'No.'

'Aunt Harriet—'

'I have spoken,' she said, rather splendidly, with a flashing gesture of the ruby which was meant to obliterate me, and did.

I gave up. 'All right, I'll tell him. He'll be glad I found you so well. Is there anything you'd like us to send you from England? Any books, for instance?'

'I can get all I want, thank you, child. Now I'm tired and you may go. Take my messages to your people, but don't think I want a spate of letters, because I don't.

I shan't answer 'em. When I'm dead John will let you know. No, you needn't kiss me. You're a pretty child and I've enjoyed your visit, so now go.'

'I've enjoyed it, too. Thank you for letting me come. Good night, Aunt Harriet.'

'Good night. John, you'll come straight back here when you've seen her to her room. Halide! Is that stupid girl going to take all night with those pills? Oh, there you are. Now don't forget what I've said, John, come straight back here.'

'Of course,' agreed Mr Lethman, sounding relieved. He already had me half-way towards the door.

For a final parting, it had the strange note of casualness which seemed exactly right. I paused for a moment in the doorway and glanced back. Halide was once more at the dressing-chest, shaking something from a small bottle into her hand. Beyond her, behind the orange glow of the lamp, the bed was towering obscurity. As she turned to mount the steps once more, something moved in the black shadows at the foot of the bed, something small and grey and quick-moving. For one flesh-creeping moment I thought there were rats even in the bedroom, but then I saw the creature leap on the bed, and the large pale hand came from behind the curtain and stroked it. A half-grown cat.

Half-wild as well. As Halide sat down on the edge of the bed the cat leaped aside and vanished. The girl, shimmering in her green silk, leaned forward towards the hidden figure of the old woman. She was offering her water in a tall, chased goblet. The scene looked like something remote and improbable, on a badly lighted stage. It could have nothing to do with me and Charles and daylight.

I turned and hurried out in the wake of John Lethman's torch.

The beam flicked upwards for a moment to light my face. 'What is it? Are you cold?'

'No. It's nothing.' I took a deep breath. 'It's wonderful to get out into the air. You were right about that tobacco, it's a bit much.'

'Was that all it was? I got the impression that the interview upset you.'

'In a way, I suppose,' I admitted. 'I must say I found it all a bit odd, and she wasn't exactly easy to talk to.'

'In what way?'

'Well, heavens—Oh, but I suppose you're used to it! I meant inconsistent, and forgetful, and the way she tried to needle me at the beginning. And – well, she *looks* so outlandish, and then that pipe . . . ! I'm afraid I was a bit tactless once or twice, but I'd always heard she hasn't much time for yes-men, and I thought it was probably best to tell the truth, flat out. I thought I'd upset her, the time she started muttering at me, but I hadn't, had I?'

'It takes more than that. Take it from me, she meant it when she said she was enjoying the conversation.'

He was, I thought, a bit curt. But any sour reflections I might have had about this were shaken as he went on: 'I wish you'd told me earlier about this cousin Charles. I might have managed to persuade her.'

'Yes, it was silly of me. I think I'd some idea of finding out first how the land lay. Is she likely to change her mind?'

'Heaven knows. Frankly, I've no idea. Once she's made a decision it's pretty hard to shift her. I sometimes feel she's obstinate just for the hell of it, if you know what I mean. I don't know why she suddenly stuck her toes in like that.'

'Neither do I. She adored him, you know – he was the only one of us she'd any use for.' I added, ruefully: 'Well, he's going to be furious with me for queering his pitch, which is what I seem to have done, goodness knows how! He's really pretty keen to see her – and not just out of curiosity like me. I don't know what he'll say. She must have talked of him to you, surely?'

'Oh, yes. If I'd only known he was here . . . Look out, mind that step. How long's he going to be in the Lebanon?'

'I've no idea.'

'Well, if he has time to spare, tell him to leave it for a few days, will you, at least till after mid-week. I'll do what I can, and get in touch with you at the Phoenicia.'

It seemed there wasn't much else I could do except trust to his good offices.

'Thank you,' I said, 'I'll tell him. When she's had time to think it over, I'm sure she'll change her mind.'

'Stranger things have happened,' said John Lethman, rather shortly.

6

Thy promises are like Adonis' gardens,
That one day bloom'd and fruitful were the
    next.

Shakespeare: *I Henry VI*

IN the night it rained.

I had got back to my room at some time between half
past one and two in the morning. The night had been
dry then, very black and perfectly still, with nothing to
suggest a storm to follow. Mr. Lethman saw me as far
as my bedroom door, where I had left the oil lamp lit,
said good night, and withdrew. I carried my lamp along
to the hammam, washed as well as I could in a trickle of
cold water, and then went back to my room again.
There was no key, but I saw a heavy wooden bar on the
inside of the door. I dropped this carefully into its
sockets. Then I took off my outer clothing, turned my
lamp down rather inexpertly and blew out the wicks,
and climbed into bed.

Even though the hour was late, and I was tired, I lay
awake for some little time turning the recent scene over
and over in my head. I imagined myself telling Charles,
telling my mother and father, and somehow none of

the words seemed to fit or be right. 'She seemed odd, she seemed ill, she's getting old, she's going to town a bit on this recluse thing—' none of these phrases seemed to fit the decidedly off-beat tone of the interview. And if she really was going to refuse to see Charles . . .

Well, that was Charles's problem, not mine. I slept.

I'm not sure whether it was the flash of lightning or the almost simultaneous crack of thunder that woke me, but as I stirred in bed and opened my eyes the sound of rain seemed to obliterate all else. I have never heard such rain. There was no wind with it, only the cracking of thunder and the vivid white rents in the black sky. I sat up in bed to watch. The window-arches flickered dramatically against the storm outside, and the portcullis squares of the grille stamped themselves on the room over and over again with their violently angled perspectives of black and white. Through the window that I had opened the scents of flowers came almost storming in, vividly wakened by the rain. With the scents came, more palpably, a good deal of the rain itself, hitting the sill and splashing on the floor in great hammering drops.

Reluctantly, I got out of bed and padded in my bare feet across the chilly floor to shut the casement. Even while I groped in momentary darkness for the catch, my arm was soaked almost to the shoulder by the slashing downpour. I slammed the casement shut, and while I fought to fix the stiff and squeaking catch I heard, from the direction of the main gate, the sudden keening howl of a big dog.

It is one of the weirdest of all sounds, bringing with

it, I suppose, race memories of wolves and jackals and such, overlaid by countless legends of death and grief. The first hound's voice rose in a throbbing wail, to be joined by the long tremolo of the other. The watch-dogs, of course, upset by the storm; but I felt my hand instinctively clench stiff on the soaked iron of the window-catch, while I listened with cold prickles running over my skin. Then I jammed the thing shut and reached for my towel to rub my arm dry.

No wonder a howling dog was supposed to foretell a death . . . As I scrubbed at my wet arm and shoulder I thought of the legend Charles had reminded me of, 'gabble ratchet', the Gabriel Hounds, Death's pack hunting through the sky . . . Certainly all hell seemed to be loose up there tonight, full cry. In the old days anyone in the palace might well have believed the hounds of the storm to be crying death.

In the old days. And you'd have been superstitious then, and believed in that kind of thing. Whereas now . . . oh, nonsense, there was nothing wrong . . .

I flung the towel down and padded back to bed.

About five seconds later I discovered something a good deal more disturbing than any Gabriel Hounds. The roof was leaking. Moreover, it was leaking in the corner right above my bed.

I discovered this – it being dark, in the simplest possible way, by getting back into bed straight into the middle of a soaking patch, and by receiving at the same moment a large gout of water squarely on the back of my neck. It was followed almost immediately by another, and another . . .

I hurled myself back on to the cold marble, and started a frantic hunt for my shoes. Perversely, the lightning had stopped almost as suddenly as it had begun, and it was now quite dark. I found one shoe eventually, and stumbled about looking for the other, but couldn't find it. I would have to light the lamp. This, of course, meant finding my handbag, and the matches I hoped I was carrying – and by the time I had done this another pint of so of water would have emptied itself into my bed. I suppose it would have been sensible to drag the bed straight away from the danger point before starting the hunt for my effects, but from what I had seen of the palace appointments, I wasn't prepared to manhandle any of their furniture about the floors in the dark. So I hopped about, blasphemously groping, until I had found my matches, and then it took me another five minutes or so to manage the lighting of the oil lamp.

Once the room was lit it was the work of moments to find my other shoe and throw something on over my near-nakedness. Then I recklessly dragged the bed away from the wall. It came across the cracked marble with a dot-and-carry-one screech of broken castors. With it out of the way, the water dripped steadily on to the floor. It was only after some moments that I realized how loud the dripping was. The rain had stopped.

I went back to the window. As suddenly as if a tap had been turned off the rain had ceased. Already I could see stars. I pulled open the casement to find that in the wake of the storm had come a small erratic breeze, which was clearing the clouds and whispering among the trees of the gorge. After the chill of the soaking storm the breeze was warm, so I left the casement wide. Then I turned back to deal with my problem.

Most of the bedcovers were still dry, having been pushed back out of the way when I got out of bed myself. I heaved these off the bed, put them gingerly on the dry part of the window-seat, then, more gingerly still, turned the mattress. It was of thick horse-hair, with a fresh cover of unbleached cotton, and I could only hope that it would last me the rest of the night before the wet soaked up through it. I discarded the sodden sheet, piled the dry bedcovers back on, put out the lamp and lay down, clothes and all, to pass what remained of the night.

But not yet in sleep. The steady dripping just beside me on the marble floor seemed as loud as a drum beat. I stood it for perhaps ten minutes, then realised I would get no sleep until I stopped it. So once more I rolled out of bed, groped for and found the crumpled and soaking sheet, and put it down under the drips. In the blessed quiet that followed, another sound from outside caught my ear, and I straightened up and stood listening.

No hounds of Death now; they were quiet. This was a bird singing in the garden, full and loud and echoing from the water and the enclosing walls. Another joined it. And then a third, waterfalls of song rinsing the clear air.

I unbarred the door and padded out across the arcade.

The surface of the lake was faintly shining, lighter than the dim starlight it reflected. Spatters of rain shook intermittently from the bushes as the breeze wandered. The nightingales' song filled the garden, welling out of the tangle of soaked and glittering creepers.

A pair of white pigeons rocketed out from their roost in the western arcade and vanished with a clap of wings over my head. Something – someone – moved in the darkness beneath the arches. A man, walking along under the arcade. He was moving very softly, and above the noise of the birds and the rustle of the leaves I couldn't hear him, but this was no white-robed Arab. It must be John Lethman. Probably he'd come along to see how I'd made out in the storm.

I waited a few moments longer, but he didn't come, and I saw nothing more. The garden, but for the song of the nightingales, was quiet and still.

I shivered suddenly. Five minutes' *Nachtmusik* was more than enough. I padded back into my room, crossly shut my door against the nightingales, and rolled back on to the bed.

I woke to blazing sunlight and a tapping on the door.

It was Halide with my breakfast, a plate of thin unleavened bread, some cream cheese, the inevitable apricot jam, and a big pot of coffee. The girl looked tired, and still eyed me sideways with that sulky glance, but made no comment on the disorder of the room, the sodden sheet on the floor, or even the bed shifted four feet out from the wall. When I thanked her for the tray and said something about the wild night, she only nodded sullenly and went out.

But everything else was cheerful this morning, even the hammam, with sunlight pouring down through the blue and amber glass bells in the ceiling, and lighting the alabaster basins and pale marble walls in a swimming subaqueous light. The water trickled – colder than ever – out of a dolphin's mouth into a silver shell. I rinsed my face and hands, went back to my room and dressed, then carried the tray out into the blazing sunshine at the edge of the pool.

The golden heat, the high blue sky, made it difficult to remember last night's storm of pouring rain, but here and there on the path where the flagstones had sunk, or in the wells dug round the tree-roots to catch the rain, the water still stood glittering, inches deep. The weeds between the stones looked already half as long again, the flowers brighter, the bushes glossy and refreshed. Even the water of the pool looked clearer, and beside it a peacock stood studying his reflection, with his tail fully spread, looking entirely artificial, like something from a picture-book, or a jewelled bird by Fabergé. Some other bird, small and golden, flirted over a rose laurel. The little kiosk on the island, freshly washed, showed a gilded dome and a glimpse of bright blue tiling. One of the nightingales was doing overtime in the roses.

I wondered how John Lethman had got in and out last night, and why.

He came some half hour later. Whatever excursions he had undertaken during the night, they didn't seem to have affected him. He looked alert and wide awake, the blurred look gone from his eyes, which were clear grey, and very bright. He moved with energetic precision, and greeted me almost gaily.

'Good morning.'

'Oh, hullo. Nice timing.' I emerged from my door with my luggage – a handbag – packed and ready. 'I was just coming to look for you and hoping the dogs had been shut up.'

'Always by day. Did they wake you last night? It was a bit rough, I'm afraid. Did you sleep through it?' Here his eyes went past me to the disorder of the room. 'I say, rough was the right word, wasn't it? What happened? Don't tell me – the roof leaked?'

'It certainly did.' I laughed. 'Did you decide to rate me third class after all? No, I'm only joking, I shifted the bed and managed quite a bit of sleep in the end. But I'm afraid you'll find the mattress pretty wet.'

'That doesn't matter, it'll dry in five minutes once it's put outside. I'm terribly sorry, the roof gutter must be blocked again. Nasirulla swore he'd cleaned it. Did you really sleep?'

'Fine, thanks, in the end. Don't worry, just think it's an ill wind that blows no good.'

'Meaning?'

'If I hadn't come turning the household upside down, you'd have been the one under the water-spout.'

'You've got something there. But believe me, you're no ill wind. Your aunt was quite set up last night after your visit.'

'Was she really? I didn't tire her?'

'Not a bit. She kept me talking quite a time after you'd gone.'

'No change about Charles, I suppose?'

'Not yet, I'm afraid, but give her time. You're ready, are you? Shall we go?' We moved towards the gate.

'Did she keep you very late?' I asked. 'It seems hard, the way you burn the torch at both ends.'

'Not very, no. I'd gone to bed before the storm broke.'

'It woke you, I suppose?'

'Not a flicker.' He laughed. 'And don't think I'm neglecting my duty, will you? Your great-aunt thrives on disturbances like last night's. She tells me she enjoyed it. She'd have made a wonderful Katisha.'

'"*But to him who's scientific There's nothing that's terrific In the falling of a flight of thunderbolts*"?' I quoted, and heard him laugh again, softly, to himself. 'Well, she's got a point, I rather enjoyed it myself. At least, I enjoyed the aftermath. The garden looked wonderful.'

I caught a quick sideways glance. 'You went out?'

'Only for a moment; I went out to listen to the nightingales. Oh, look at the flowers! Is that because of the storm? More good from the ill wind, would you say?'

We were crossing the small courtyard where Hamid and I had waited yesterday. Here, too, the rain had washed the place clean, and the marble pillars dazzled white in the sun. At their feet the carved troughs were a blaze of red anemones, wide open and shiny as fresh blood in the long grass.

'My Adonis Gardens,' said Mr Lethman.

'Your what?'

'Adonis Gardens. I suppose you know the Adonis myth?'

'I know Aphrodite met him in the Lebanon and he died there, and that every spring his blood stains the river and it runs red to the sea. What is it, iron in the water?'

'Yes. It's one of the spring resurrection stories, like Persephone, or the Osiris myth. Adonis was a corn-god, a fertility god, and he dies to rise again. The "Adonis Gardens" are – you might call them little personal symbols of death and resurrection; and they're sympathetic magic as well, because the people who planted them and forced the seeds and flowers to grow as quickly as they could, thought they were helping the year's harvest. The flowers and herbs sprang up and withered and died all in a few days, and then the "gardens" with the images of the god were taken, with the women wailing and mad with grief, down to the sea and thrown in. See? It was all mixed up, here, with the Dionysiac cult, and Osiris, and the rites of Attis, and it still persists – only in nice, pure forms! – all over the world, believe it or not.' He checked, with a glance at me. 'Sorry, rather a lecture.'

'I'm interested, no, go on. Why did you plant the gardens here?'

'No reason, except that this is the right time of the year, and it's quite interesting to see how quickly they do spring up and die, here in Adonis's own valley. Wouldn't you say so?'

'*I* would, sure. It's the kind of romantic notion that

appeals to me like anything. But why to you? I mean, what have Adonis and Co. got to do with psychological medicine? Or is this Aunt Harriet's idea?'

'With—? Oh, didn't I tell you I was writing a paper? I was interested in the psychology of religious possession, and I'm touching on some aspects of the ecstatic religions of the near East – the Orphic myth and Dionysius and the Adonis story in its various forms. That's all. I've got some quite interesting stuff locally.' He grinned, perhaps a little shamefacedly. 'I haven't really let it slide, you know. Whenever I'm let off the chain I ride out and up into the hill villages. If you stay hereabouts for long you may—'

'Ride?'

We were in the *midan* now, the big entrance court. He nodded across it. 'There's still a horse here. You know your great-aunt used to ride until only a couple of years ago? She really is remarkable – Hullo! The door's still shut. Nasirulla's not come over yet.' He glanced at his watch. 'He's late. Half a minute while I open it and give Kasha some air.'

He pulled open the upper half-door, and latched it back to the wall with a rotten-looking wooden peg. In the dim interior a horse stood dozing, head down and ears relaxed. A chestnut Arab.

'Do you wear Arab dress when you ride?' I asked.

He looked surprised. 'Usually, yes. It's cooler. Why? Wait a minute – didn't you say you'd gone to the Adonis Source yesterday? Did you see me up there?'

'Yes, at some village beyond the fall. I recognised the horse. You had the dogs with you.' I smiled. 'You looked terribly romantic, especially with the salukis, I may tell you, you made my day.'

'And now I've spoiled the picture? Not an Arab Emir after all with his hawk and his hounds after gazelle, just a drifter who's found a lazy billet in the sun and will probably never have the *nous* to pull out of it.'

I didn't answer, for the simple reason that I couldn't think how to. The words were bitter, but were spoken without a bitter tinge; and even if I had wanted to, there was no comforting reply to make. John Lethman must know as well as I did that his job, such as it was, would expire with Great-Aunt Harriet. Or would it? Was he actually playing for Dar Ibrahim itself, and a 'lazy billet in the sun' here eventually on his own? He had said it was a 'wonderful place to write in', and however I might disagree with him, I could think of worse places for an unambitious man to settle in, for a dilettante life in a delightful climate, and with a houri thrown in . . . It might be that the dilapidation of the palace was due, not to lack of money, but to age and indifference. John Lethman might well be aware – none better – what means there would eventually be, not only to run part of the place comfortably, but to escape from it at need. Not a bad billet at all.

We were at the gate. There was no sign of Jassim, so Mr Lethman pulled back the heavy bolts and opened the bronze door. Outside, the sun blazed down white on the stony plateau. There was no one there.

'Your driver isn't here yet,' he said. 'If you'd rather come back in and wait—'

'Thanks very much, but I think I'll just walk down to meet him. And thank you for all you've done, Mr Lethman.' I held out my hand and he took it, but when I would have gone on he protested very pleasantly that both he and Great-Aunt Harriet had enjoyed the visit very much.

'And I really will do what I can about your cousin, but if I can't' – he hesitated, and the light eyes met mine and slid away – 'I hope you won't feel too badly about it.'

'I? It's none of my business. How she lives is her own affair, and if Charles is really set on seeing her it's up to him to find a way. Goodbye then, and thanks again. And I hope the paper goes well.'

'Goodbye.'

The big door shut. The palace had sealed itself off once more behind me, silent walls of baked stone throwing back the glare from the white rock underfoot. In front of me the valley stretched in all the hard brilliance of morning.

The sun was behind me, and the cliff path was in shadow. Here, too, the effect of last night's rain was immediately apparent. Even the rock smelled fresher, and the dust had caked into mud which was drying rapidly into a million cracks. I could have sworn that on some of the fig trees that clung to the face of the rock there were fresh green buds. I wondered if, when I got down to the foot of the cliff, I would see Hamid crossing to meet me.

But there was no sign of him, and when I reached the Nahr el-Sal'q I saw why. The river was in spate.

The ill wind had been at work here, too, and this time to no good that I could see at all. There must have been, high up in the catchment area, as heavy a fall as, if not heavier than, that which we had had in the valley. It may even have combined with melting snow on the high tops to come pouring down now into the valley, for the Nahr el-Sal'q seemed to have risen at least two feet, and to be coming down very fast indeed. Where yesterday afternoon the pile of stone that had flanked the old Roman bridge had stood at least a foot clear of water, now there was nothing to be seen but the angry white of broken water as the river, streaked with red mud, cascaded down to meet the Adonis.

There is something in all of us which cannot quite accept so sudden a reversal of circumstance. It did not seem possible that I could really be cut off on the wrong side of the river. It should be still as it was yesterday, swift but clear, and easily to be crossed if one could find the place. I stood there on the rocky edge which, this morning, seemed barely to clear the rushing level of the water, and stared about me rather helplessly. This must be why Nasirulla hadn't turned up for work this morning. Even if Hamid did come for me – and there was as yet no sign of him – he couldn't cross the river any more than I could. I was nicely imprisoned here between the roaring stream of the Nahr el-Sal'q and the still bigger torrent of the Adonis. Unless I could make my way up the valley between the two, and cross somewhere where the stream was a good deal narrower, I was certainly marooned. I supposed that, once the spate began to subside, it would fall as quickly as it had risen, but I had no means of knowing how soon this might be.

Meanwhile Hamid would certainly come to seek me from the village, so there was nothing much to do but sit beside the stream and wait for his appearance. Behind me the palace, standing back from the head of the cliff, was invisible, but ahead I had a clear view of the village strung high along the valley's edge. I looked about me, found a flat boulder washed beautifully clean by the night's rain, and sat down to wait.

It was then that I saw the boy.

There had been no movement; that I could swear. One moment, it seemed to me, I had been gazing idly at the torrential water and beyond it a stony bank full in the sun and ornamented with a few harsh green shrubs. The next moment I found myself looking straight at the boy, sturdy and ragged in his rustic kaftan, who could have been anything from twelve to fifteen years old. He was barefooted, and unlike most of the Arab boys that one saw, his head also was bare, covered with a shock of wild dark hair. His skin was dark brown. He was standing stock-still beside a bush, leaning on a thick stick.

He seemed to be staring straight at me. After a moment's hesitation I got off my boulder and picked my way back to the river's edge. The boy didn't move.

'Hullo there! Do you speak English?' My voice whirled away and was drowned in the roar of the water between us, and I raised it and tried again. 'Can you hear me?'

He nodded. It was a curiously dignified nod, the sort

of gesture one might have expected from an actor, not from a herd-boy. That this is what he was I now saw; one or two of the goats that we had seen yesterday were moving slowly and at random down the slope behind him, cropping at the thin flowers as they came. Then with a movement that was all small boy, and not dignified at all, he thrust his stick into the stony earth, and pole-vaulted down towards his side of the stream. Now we were barely twenty feet apart, but with all the roaring of the Nahr el-Sal'q between us.

I tried again. 'Where can I cross the water?'

This time he shook his head. 'Tomorrow.'

'I didn't say *when*, I said *where*!' But he had, in fact, answered my question. The implication was clear. The crossing place, probably the only crossing place, was here, and the river would take twenty-four hours to go down.

My dismay must have been obvious. He waved with the stick upstream towards the towering cliffs that barred the head of the valley, and then down to where the two rivers rushed together in a wrangle of white foam stained with red. 'Bad,' he shouted, 'all bad! You stay there!' A sudden smile, very boyish, showing two gaps in the even white teeth, 'You stay with the Lady, huh? Your father's father's sister?'

'My . . . ?' I worked it out yet again. He was right. And it was Nasirulla, of course, everyone in the village would know all about it by now. 'Yes. You live in the village?'

A gesture, not to the village, but to the barren landscape and the goats. 'I live here.'

'Can you get a mule? A donkey?' I had thought of John Lethman's horse, but somehow that would be a last resort. 'I would pay well!' I shouted.

That shake of the head again. 'No mule. Donkey, too small. You all drown. This is a bad river.' After some thought he added in explanation: 'There was rain in the night.'

'You must be joking.'

He got the meaning, even though he couldn't have heard me. The gap-toothed grin flashed again, and then he pointed towards the village. I hadn't seen him look that way, but when I looked myself I saw Hamid, a slim figure in dark blue trousers and steel-blue shirt, detach himself from the dense shadow under the retaining wall that held the village to the cliff top, and start on his way down the path.

I turned back to the boy.

The goats were there, still grazing: the river roared; the distant village wavered on the cliff top in the heat; but down here on the rocky bank there was no sign of any boy. Only the liquid rocks shimmering up in the heat, and where he had been standing a shaggy black goat, staring at me with those cold yellow eyes.

A country where anything could happen.

'By all the gods at once,' I said aloud, 'I could do with your keeping that promise, cousin dear, here and now, and no kidding.'

Some ten seconds later I realised that the small figure in the distance was not Hamid at all, but Charles himself, coming fast down the slope towards me.

7

While smooth Adonis from his native rock
Ran purple to the sea . . .

Milton: *Paradise Lost*

CERTAINLY a country where anything could happen.
After my disturbed night among the storybook para-
phernalia of the palace – peacocks, mute servants,
harem gardens – no touch of magic would have surprised me. What did faintly surprise me was that I
should so immediately have distinguished Charles at
such a distance from Hamid, whom I had been expecting. So immediately – and with such a calm uprush
of pleasure.

I sat still on my boulder in the sun, watching
him.

When he was still some way off, he raised a
hand to greet me, then something seemed to catch
his attention, for he paused and turned, apparently
to address a patch of shade under a dusty bush.
As I watched, the patch of shade revolved into a
black goat, and squatting down cross-legged beside
it the herd-boy, his stick lying at his feet in the
dust.

The conversation lasted a minute or two, then the boy got to his feet, and the two of them came down together towards the river bank.

I walked down again to my side, and we stood surveying one another across the twenty feet of turbid, red-streaked water.

'Hi!' said Charles.

'Hi!' I shouted. Then, not very brilliantly: 'We're stuck. It's in spate.'

'So it seems, Serves you right. Stealing a march. How's Great-Aunt H?'

'Fine. You're early. How did you manage?'

'Made it this morning. Hotel told me. Saw your driver this morning, told him I'd fetch you.'

'You did? Fine, you go right ahead and fetch me! . . . Oh, Charles, the boy says it'll be in spate till tomorrow. What are we going to do?'

'I'll come over,' said my cousin.

'You can't! It's hellish deep. Did you get rain last night in Beirut?'

'Did I get what?'

'Rain?' I gestured to a flawless sky. 'Rain?'

'I can't think why we're standing twenty feet apart talking about the weather,' said Charles, starting to undo his shirt buttons.

I yelled in alarm: 'Charles, you can't! And it wouldn't help if you did—'

'You can watch or not as you please,' said my cousin. 'Remember the good old days when we used to be dumped in the bath together? Don't worry, I'll manage this lot.'

'I can hardly wait to watch you drown,' I said tartly. 'But if you'd only *listen*—'

He stopped unbuttoning and turned a look of inquiry. 'Yes?'

I threw a quick glance over my shoulder. It seemed all wrong to be standing yelling about our private affairs in the middle of the valley, but all I could see was the tangle of bushes and trees on the cliff behind me. The palace was out of sight, and nothing moved on the path.

I shouted: 'It won't do you any good if you do get across, She says she won't see you.'

'Won't see me?'

I nodded.

'Why not?'

I made a gesture. 'Can't tell you here. But she won't.'

'Well, then, when?'

'Never – she meant not at all. She won't see anyone at all. Charles, I'm sorry—'

'She actually told you that?'

'Yes, and she seemed a bit—' Here my throat, sore with yelling, made me stop and cough.

I saw Charles make a movement of intense irritation, then he turned to the boy who was standing just behind him closely attended by the black goat. I had forgotten all about him. I somehow hadn't counted him as an audience to our conversation, any more than the goats, or the rocks and stones into which he could apparently melt at will.

From the boy's gestures, aided by his pointing stick, it seemed clear what Charles was asking him. And presently my cousin turned back to me and raised his voice again.

'He says I can cross farther up.'

'He told me there wasn't anywhere.'

'Still one or two things I can do that you can't,' he retorted. 'Anyway . . . hopeless . . . can't stand here yelling intimacies about Aunt H. across twenty feet of flood water.' A gesture indicated the palace, invisible above me at the cliff top. 'Right underneath . . . hellish row . . . And I've got to talk to you. Ahmad says there's a place upstream. Can you make it your side?'

'I'll try.'

I turned and began to make my way up my side of the stream. There was no path, and here the water ran close under the cliff, so the going was rough, and complicated by a fairly thick growth of scrubby bushes and small trees. Soon I lost sight of Charles and his guide as I battled my way among bushes and rocks, intent on nothing but keeping my feet.

The Nahr el-Sal'q seemed to flow for most of this part of its length in a gully fairly thickly grown with trees. These, and the broken terrain, made it impossible to stay always within sight of the water. I caught one or two more glimpses of Charles and the boy, then they vanished, apparently following some winding goat-track up into the thickets.

I clambered on along my side of the gully for some half mile, to find the stream then curving and its bed shelving steeply up into a narrower gorge where the water dropped from pool to pool in a series of rapids, running deep and fast. Charles and the boy reappeared here, their path apparently clinging close above the torrent, but though the stream was narrow here, and everywhere full of rocks, there was still no place where it seemed safe to cross. And the narrower the gully the faster and louder grew the water, so that any kind of communication, other than by gesture, was impossible.

The boy kept pointing upstream in an Excelsior kind of way. Charles spread his hands to me and jerked an encouraging thumb. We toiled on, separated by the loud white rush of water.

It must have been after a full mile of painful going that the stream-bed took a sudden and final lift and curve, and ran, in a manner of speaking, right up against the cliff.

In fact, of course, the stream came straight out of the cliff. The spring which fed the Nahr el-Sal'q was almost a miniature of the Adonis Source, leaping suddenly into the sunlight from a gash in the dry rock face that blocked the upper end of the gully. It was much smaller, less dramatic, and much less haunted. The spring, a spout of ice-green water, jetted out of the cliff with a roar that the echoes magnified, tossed itself into a churning pool, then went tearing off down among the white boulders of the gully. A few hanging bushes, soaked and ragged with the spray, waved in the breeze of the fall. The sun drove against the cliff where the water gushed, lighting the cascade into glittering brilliance, but below, where we stood, the place was in shadow and the wind off the water struck chilly.

I stared about me with dismay. If communication had been difficult down at the ford, and worse in the gully, here it was impossible. The roar of the water, magnified a dozen times by its echoes, bellowed round from rock to rock so that, though Charles and I were here barely eight or nine feet apart, we could not have heard a word the other spoke. Moreover, I could still see no way across. To cross the torrent here would have been suicide, and above the cascade towered a seamed and sunlit crag as high as a cathedral.

It was at this that the boy was pointing, and presently, to my alarm, I saw Charles approaching it. My yell of protest, or perhaps my wild gesture, reached him, for he stopped, nodded his head at me, jerked a thumbs-up gesture, then with apparent confidence approached the cliff. Only then did I remember that rock-climbing had been another of the ploys with which (*vide* my father) my cousin had been wont to waste his time all over Europe. I relaxed. All I could do was hope that Charles had, as he usually did (*vide* my mother), wasted his time to good effect.

It seemed he had. I have no idea whether it was in fact an easy climb, or whether he simply made it seem so, but there was very little to it. He went carefully, because in places the rock was wet or loose, but it was not long before he had gained my side of the Nahr el-Sal'q. He came down the last pitch at no more than a scramble, to land safely beside me.

'Hullo, Aphrodite.'

'Adonis, I presume? Nice to see you, but if you've any idea of guiding my tottering steps back across the north wall of the Eiger with you, you can have another think. It's not on.'

'I wouldn't risk my own precious neck trying. No, I'm afraid you're stuck, sweet coz. It's beastly cold down here, isn't it, and there's still a hellish noise . . . Shall we get up into the sun where we can talk?'

'For goodness' sake, yes, let's. I must say it seems a lot of trouble to go to, just to have a little conversation.'

'Ah, not with you,' said my cousin. 'Wait a moment, I'll tell the boy – where is he? Did you see him go?'

'Haven't you guessed? That's not a boy, that's a faun. He's invisible at will.'

'Very likely,' agreed Charles calmly. 'Well, he'll turn up when he wants his tip.'

I followed him out of the gully, and we soon emerged on a small stony plateau where the sun struck hotly.

Here, too, the resemblance to the Adonis Source was underlined, for on the plateau stood the tumbled ruins of some ancient temple. Nothing remained now but the steep steps of the portico, a stretch of broken floor, and two standing pillars. It must only have been a small place originally, perhaps a subordinate shrine of the greater Gods of Afka, built at the tributary source, and it was weedy, forgotten, and undramatic. Tufts of some yellow flower grew between the stones, and half-way up one pillar where the masonry had fallen into a crumbling hole, a hawk had made an untidy nest liberally streaked with white droppings; but somehow the squared masculine-looking Roman stones, the honey-coloured pillars, the pitted steps where the thistles grew, fitted with a kind of beauty into that wild landscape.

The steps provided a seat for us in the shade of one

of the pillars. The roar of the cascade was cut off by the sides of the gorge, and the silence was intense.

Charles got out cigarettes and offered one to me.

'No, thanks. Oh, Charles, I'm awfully glad you came! What am I going to do? I can't climb across that awful rock, and the faun told me the water wouldn't go down till tomorrow.'

'So I gather. Actually there is another way. He tells me there's some kind of track going up into the heights near Afka, but it's a hell of a way, and if I was to take the car up by road to meet you you'd have to go on your own, and you'd never find it. I suppose the boy might manage to cross and act as guide for you, but we'd still probably never manage an RV in a million years. The place is seamed with tracks.'

'And probably creeping with wild boars and yelling tribes of Midian or whatever. Nothing,' I said flatly, 'will get me clambering up into the High Lebanon, boy or no boy.'

'How I agree.' My cousin leaned back lazily against the pillar and blew smoke at the sun. 'If the water doesn't go down again before night there's only one thing to do, go back to the palace.' He slanted a look at me, eyebrows raised. 'That's certainly what I was hoping to do. What's all this about her not letting me in?'

'Just that she said she wouldn't, and as a matter of fact I'm not wild keen to go back there myself. I'll tell you about that in a minute . . . But look, I couldn't make out just what you were yelling at me down by the ford – you did say you'd seen Hamid, didn't you, my driver? He was to have come for me this morning.'

'Yes, I saw him, and it's all right, I came instead. You knew Ben's father was delayed and couldn't get home till Sunday – yesterday? Well, he telephoned again last night to say he couldn't make it, had to go on to Aleppo and possibly Homs, and wasn't sure when he'd get home, so I told Ben I'd go back there later, but I wanted to come straight up to Beirut while you were here. I didn't try telephoning you last night because it was pretty late when he called, and I left first thing this morning – and I mean first thing, literally crack of dawn. There wasn't a thing on the road, and I came up the Barada Valley at the speed of sound, and the frontier post let me through in twenty minutes, which must be an all-time record for them. I got to Beirut about eight o'clock. Your driver was in the hotel lobby when I checked in and asked about you, and he told me you were staying the night here and he'd promised to come and fetch you. So I told him not to bother, I'd come straight up myself.'

'As long as he hasn't lost another contract by giving me the day.'

'Not to worry, I paid him,' said Charles. 'I'm darned sure he'll get another contract anyway, the Phoenicia's always full of streams of people wanting cars. He seemed pretty pleased.'

'That's all right, then. He's a very nice chap, as a matter of fact. I had a lovely day yesterday.'

Charles tapped ash off into a clump of weeds. 'That's what I've come to hear about. After all the trouble we've gone to to have a little conversation, it'd better be good. What the devil do you mean by stealing a march on me, young Christy? Was Aunt H so disgusted with you that she refused to see anybody else?'

'Probably.' I sat up. 'Oh, my dear, there's masses to tell you! Actually, I'd no real intention of calling at the palace, but when we got to the village Hamid stopped the car, and it looked so near, sort of weird and romantic, and of course it never occurred to me really that she'd refuse to see either of us. Look, away down there, see? You can actually see it from here, too. It looks rather gorgeous, doesn't it? I must say distance lends enchantment! Close to it's just about dropping to bits.'

You could indeed, from this high eyrie, see the end of the promontory on which the palace stood. As the eagle flew, it cannot have been much more than three-quarters of a mile distant, and in the clean and brilliant air even the branches of the feathery trees were clearly visible.

We were looking down on the back of the palace. I could see the high blank wall and inside it the flower-roofed arches enclosing the glint of the lake. Beyond the Seraglio sprawled the jumble of roofs and court-yards whose geography, even now, I couldn't guess at. From the distance the palace looked completely deserted, like a ruin open to the sun.

'See the green courtyard and the lake?' I said. 'That's the Seraglio where I slept.'

'How appropriate,' said Charles. 'And Aunt H?'

'She has the Prince's Court.'

'She would. Well, tell me all about it. Hamid told me

you rather took them by surprise, but you got in in the end.'

' "In the end" is right, and I didn't get to Aunt H till about midnight.'

I told him my story then, omitting nothing that I could remember.

He heard me out to the end without much interruption. Then he stirred, dropped the stub of his cigarette carefully beside his foot on the stone, and crushed it out. He regarded me frowningly.

'Quite a story, eh? Well, we expected a queer situation, didn't we? But it's queerer even than you think.'

'Meaning?'

He asked flatly: 'Did she strike you as sane?'

I have often read about moments of 'revelation'. These seemed to be sudden – blinding lights on the Damascus road, scales dropping from eyes, and so forth. I hadn't ever thought about it much, except to class it vaguely as a 'miracle', a thing that happened in the Bible or some other lofty context, and not normally – not in real life – at all. But in a minor and very personal way, I had a revelation now.

There was my cousin, the same boy I had known for twenty-two years, looking at me and asking a question. I had known him ever since I could remember. I had shared the bath with him. I had seen him smacked. I had jeered at him when he fell off the orchard wall and cried. I had discussed sex with him at the age when we had no physical secrets from one another. Later, when we had, I had regarded him with a tolerant and familiar indifference. Meeting him the other day in Straight

Street I had been pleased, but not bowled over with delight.

And now, here, suddenly, he turned his head and looked at me and asked a question, and I saw, as if I had never seen them before, the grey long-lashed eyes, the well-cut hair growing thick and smooth, the faint hollow under the cheek-bones, the slightly arrogant and wholly exciting cut of nostril and upper lip, the whole vivid intelligence and humour and force of the man's face.

'What's the matter?' he asked, irritably.

'Nothing. What did you say?'

'I asked you if Aunt H struck you as sane.'

'Oh.' I pulled myself together. 'Yes, of course she did! I told you she was odd and woolly and said she forgot things, and she was really quite sharp and nasty in a way, but . . .' I hesitated. 'I can't quite explain what I mean, but I do know she *looked* sane. However peculiar she was, and the way she was dressed and everything . . . Charles, her eyes were sane.'

He nodded. 'That's what I mean. No, wait, you haven't heard my side of it yet.'

'Your side of it? You mean you've heard something more since we last met?'

'Indeed and indeed. I rang my people up on Friday evening to tell them I was leaving Damascus soon for Beirut. I told them I'd met you, and that we were going to spend two or three days together and we were coming up to see Great-Aunt H. I wondered if they had any messages to send, or anything like that. Well, my mother said they'd had a letter from her.'

I looked at him, startled. 'A letter? Do you mean another Will or something?'

'No, a letter. It came about three weeks ago, while I was in North Africa. Must have been just after you left. My mother had actually written to tell me about it, and when I phoned she told me her letter would be waiting for me care of Cook's in Beirut. What's more, she'd forwarded Aunt H's letter to me there.' His hand went to his inside pocket.

'You've got it?'

'I picked it up this morning. Wait till you've read it and then tell me if it makes sense to you.'

He handed me the letter. It was written on coarse-looking paper which could have been some sort of torn-off wrapping, and the handwriting was spidery and spluttery as though it had been written with a quill pen; which in fact it probably had. But it was perfectly legible.

My dear Nephew,

Last month I recd a letter from my dear Husband's friend and colleague Humphrey Ford who you will remember was with us in Resada in 1949 and again in '53 and '54. He tells me that he recently recd the news from a Friend that my Gt-Nephew, yr son Charles, is at present studying the languages of the East with a view (he thinks) to adopting my dear Husband's profession. Poor Humphrey cd not be clear over this as he is getting sadly absent, but he informed me that young Chas will be travelling this yr in

Syria. If he wishes to call on me, I shld make a
point of receiving him. As you know I do not
approve of the freedom with wch young people
are brought up nowadays, and yr son is what my
dear Mother wd have called a Scapegrace, but a
clever boy, and wd be amused to receive him.
There is much to interest him here in the study
of Eastern Life and Manners.

I do well enough here with my small Staff who
are v. attentive and a man from the village who
looks after the dogs, Samson cannot abide the
Dr. Young Chas will remember him.

Regards to yr Wife also to my other Nephew
and Wife – the little girl must be well grown by
now, a strange little thing, but like enough the
Boy to be called Handsome.

Yr affec Aunt,

Harriet Boyd.

Post Scriptum – The Times continues flimsy so
that I cannot believe Yr. Representations were
sufficiently decided.

Post Post Scriptum. I have purchased an
excellent Tombstone locally.

I read through the letter once, then clean through again,
more slowly, and I think my mouth must have been wide
open all the time. Then I gaped up at my cousin. He was
leaning back against the pillar, head back, eyes narrowed
under the long lashes, watching me.

'Well?'

'But Charles . . . when did she – is it dated? There's a squiggle at the top but I can't read it.'

'Arabic,' he said shortly. 'Written in February. From the postmark it looks as if she didn't get it mailed straight off, and she didn't send it airmail, so it took nearly three weeks on the way. But that's not the point. It was certainly written after Christmas's Last Will and Testament. Would you or would you not say that was an open invitation?'

'I certainly would. Two months ago? Well, obviously something's happened to make her change her mind.'

'John Lethman?'

'D'you think that's possible?' I asked.

'Not having seen the ménage, I wouldn't know. What's he like?'

'Tallish and rather thin, and slouches a bit. Light eyes—'

'My dear girl, I'm reasonably indifferent to him physically. Would you say he was honest?'

'How do I know?'

' "No art to find the mind's construction in the face?" Well, I agree, of course, but what was your impression?'

'Not a bad one. I told you he was a bit off-putting at first, but if Hamid's right he wasn't back on the beam properly, and in any case it's obvious he was only doing what Aunt H had told him to. After he'd seen her he was all right. She probably told him he'd nothing to fear from that strange little thing, however much she resembled the handsome boy.'

He didn't smile. 'Then you did think he might be feathering his nest?'

'The thought had crossed my mind,' I admitted, 'once Hamid put it there. We both agreed we had unpleasant natures. Does it matter?'

'Hardly, as long as it's her idea as well as his.'

'I don't think you need worry about that. I got the impression that she did exactly as she liked about a hundred per cent of the time. I doubt if he could stop her doing anything she'd set her heart on.'

'So long as that's true . . .'

'I swear it. You know, there's no sense in trying to build up something out of nothing. She simply changed her mind since she wrote that letter. It's perfectly possible she really had forgotten how devastating you were. People do.'

'You must tell me about it some time.' He stirred. 'Oh, God, I don't care what she's up to or how her mind's working, as long as things are going the way she wants them. It's just that she's as old as the seven hills, and alone except for this chap we know nothing about, and what you said about the hashish-smoking didn't sound too cheerful to me. He may be all right now, but he's on the road to nowhere, you must know that.' He moved again, restlessly. 'No doubt if she's lived here all this time she knows how many beans make five, and you say you got the impression she could deal with him—'

'Six of him.'

'Yes. I'd have liked to see for myself, that's all. You have to admit that last night doesn't exactly chime in with this letter of hers.'

'Would you expect it to? I wouldn't have thought consistency was her middle name.'

'No, but – she gave no reason whatever for her embargo on me?'

'None whatever. I honestly did just get the impression that, having seen me, she'd satisfied her own curiosity, and now she wanted to get back to her own life, whatever it is. I told you, she seemed perfectly normal for long periods, then she'd suddenly look as if she were miles away and say the queerest things. I've never met anyone who was cuckoo before, so I wouldn't know how to tell, but I'd have said nothing worse than old and absent-minded. All I can tell you is, I quite like John Lethman, and Aunt H did seem perfectly happy and contented and not ill, apart from wheezing a bit. But as for knowing what she was thinking about, don't forget I hardly know her at all, and in any case at the time I wasn't feeling too good myself, what with that ghastly tobacco, and the stuffy room, and that rather revolting bubbling noise she made with her pipe. Oh and Charles, I forgot completely – there was a cat in the room, and I didn't know it. It must have been behind the bed-curtains. I was feeling as queer as all-get-out, and thought it was just the stuffy room or something, but that must have been what it was.'

'*Cat*?' His head jerked away from the pillar, His turn to stare. 'Sweet Christ, was there?'

I was rather flattered than otherwise at the blasphemy. So Charles hadn't forgotten the thing I had about cats, or the real horror it was for me.

Now, a phobia can't be explained. And cat phobia – the genuine article – is something so grotesque as to be not quite believable. I admire cats; I love their looks; pictures of them give me pleasure. But I cannot be in the same room with them, and on the rare occasions when I have tried to kill my fear and touch a cat, it has almost made me ill. Cats are my nightmare. When I was a child at school my dear little friends found out about this, and shut me into a room with the school kitten. I was rescued, a screaming jelly of hysteria, twenty minutes later. It is the one vulnerable thing about me that Charles, even at his most horrible stage as a boy, never tortured me with. He doesn't share the phobia, but he is close enough to me to understand it.

I smiled at him. 'No, I haven't got over it, I don't know if one ever does. I saw it just as I was leaving the room. It sneaked out from behind the curtains and jumped on the bed beside her, and she started stroking it. It can't have been there all the time, or I'd have felt rotten earlier, and I'd have guessed. It occurred to me there must be another door into the room that I didn't notice. Stands to reason there would be, in a room that size.'

He said nothing. I went back to studying the letter in my hand. 'Who's Humphrey Ford?'

'Who? Oh the letter, yes. He's Oriental Studies, Professor Emeritus. "Sadly absent" is the *mot juste*, I may say. He had the reputation of giving the first lecture of term, then sloping quietly off to Saudi Arabia for a sort of perpetual Sabbatical. Before my time, praise be to Allah, but he was still around the place, and

had me to breakfast once or twice, and even occasionally recognised me in the street. A nice old chap.'

'Why hadn't you told her yourself you were
coming?'

'I wasn't sure when I'd get here, and I thought it
might be better to play it by ear once I was in Beirut.'

'And Samson? Is it Samson, there's a blot? The cat?'

'Dog. Tibetan terrier. She got him when she was
home last – he used to belong to one of the Boyd
cousins who died, and she scooped him up and
brought him back here as a mate for Delilah. He
was originally called Wu or Pooh or something equally
Tibetan, but she changed it to Samson, guess why.'

'Too subtle for me.' I handed the letter back. 'I never
saw the dogs, they were shut up except at night. John
Lethman said they were dangerous.'

'If Samson had taken a dislike to him, he was
probably protecting himself, not you.' He folded the
letter and put it back in his pocket. I got the impression
that he was talking slightly at random. 'He was a savage
little brute, as I remember, except with the family.
You'd have been all right: don't they say there's some
sort of family voice or smell or something that they
recognise even if they've never seen you before?'

'Do they?' I laced my fingers round a knee and
leaned back with my face lifted to the sun. 'You know,
Charles, that letter might work both ways . . . if she's
forgotten what she'd written in that letter when she saw
me, she's probably forgotten now what she said about
your not coming. See what I mean? In any case I told
you, John Lethman said he'd talk to her, and if his bona

fides are okay, he will, Even if they're not – or is it "it's"? . . . Even if it's not he'll not dare just ignore you. It sounded as if he wasn't planning to; he talked about getting in touch with you. In that case you can produce Aunt H's letter and make him let you in.'

'I suppose so.' But his voice was absent, and he was making rather a business of lighting another cigarette.

'Or look, for goodness' sake, why don't you just come back with me here and now, because I am genuinely stuck here and *have* to go back? We can show John Lethman the letter now, and see if you can't bulldoze your way in to see Aunt Harriet tonight. He can hardly stop you if you're on the very doorstep . . . Charles are you *listening*?'

I don't think he was. He was looking away from me, down the bright distance of the valley towards the palace.

'Look over there.'

At first I could see nothing except the crumbling ruin sleeping in the heat, the fixed dazzling pattern of the rock seamed with violent shadows, the green of distant trees greyed by the heat haze. There were no clouds to move, or wind to move them, No sound.

Then I saw what he was watching. Some way from the palace, among the rocks and tangled bushes that marked the lip of the Adonis gorge, there was a movement which presently resolved itself into a man in Arab dress making his way slowly on foot towards the palace. He was almost indistinguishable from the countryside, for his dress was dust-coloured, and his headcloth brown, and if Charles and I had not both had abnormally long sight I doubt if we would have seen him at all. He moved very slowly, disappearing from time to time as his path took him behind rocky outcrops or through the thick undergrowth, but presently he emerged on the open rock of the plateau behind the palace. He carried a stick in one hand, and seemed to have some kind of bag over his shoulder.

'Looks like a pilgrim,' I said. 'Well, he's in for a disappointment if he's making for the palace, and I don't see where else he could be bound for. The faun must be right, there's a path there.'

'There'd have to be, wouldn't there?' said my cousin. 'Did it never occur to you to wonder how John Lethman got back to the palace before you did yesterday?'

'Silly of me, I never thought of it. Yes, and I remember now, there was something about the palace being on the old camel route down from the High Lebanon to the sea. In that case there must be a reasonable track.' I grinned at him. 'But not, Charles my love, not for me.'

'On the contrary,' said my cousin, 'I'm beginning to think – Just a minute, keep your eye on that man.'

The 'pilgrim' had reached the back wall of the palace, but instead of turning north to skirt the Seraglio wall, he went the other way, making for the corner where the walls literally grew out of the cliffs of the Adonis gorge. There was a clump of trees marking the drop, and into these he vanished.

'But he can't get round that way!' I exclaimed. 'That's the way my bedroom looked. It's a sheer drop into the river.'

'He's got a rendezvous,' said Charles.

I narrowed my eyes against the brightness. Then I saw them among the trees, the Arab, and another man with him, this one in European dress. They came out slowly between the trees, obviously deep in talk, and stood there, tiny foreshortened figures at the edge of the dappled shade.

'John Lethman?' asked Charles.

'Must be. Look there's someone else, I'm sure I saw someone else move among those trees. In white, this time.'

'Yes, another Arab. That'll be your doorman, Jassim, I suppose.'

'Or Nasirulla – oh no, I'd forgotten, he couldn't get over today. Then it must be Jassim.' I knitted my brows. 'I don't understand, have they been waiting out there for him all this time? I haven't been watching, particularly, but if they'd come round from the front gate, you'd think we'd have seen them.'

'There is a way round?'

'Yes, round the north side below the Seraglio arcade. The path goes through the trees above the Nahr el-Sal'q and skirts the palace wall.'

'If they'd come that way we'd certainly have seen them. No, it's obvious there must be a back door. Stands to reason there would be. It must be hidden somewhere among those trees.'

'Tradesman's entrance?' I said. 'I suppose you're right. Look, he's handed over his pack, whatever it is. He's going now. Will they see us if they look this way?'

'Not a hope. We're in the shadow of this pillar, and what's more, the sun will be in their eyes. I wish we had a pair of field-glasses, I'd like to see your Mr. Lethman. Yes, he's going. Watch the others. My bet is we'll never see them disappear.'

Made tiny by distance, the little scene had a silent, curiously dreamlike quality. One moment there seemed to be three men standing beside the trees below the wall, then the next moment the travelling Arab had turned and was making his slow way back among the rocks, and the other two had vanished under the shade of the trees.

We waited in silence. The Arab had gone, the other two did not come out from the grove. There must indeed be another way into the palace. The distance was clear, the colours bright, but it still looked a very long way away. I thought with weariness, and then with irritation, of the long trek back down the gorge of the Nahr el-Sal'q.

I said suddenly: 'I quite honestly don't want to go back there. Can't we scrub it?'

'Decided you'd rather try the pilgrims' way into the High Lebanon?'

'No, but couldn't you somehow convey me across the Eiger after all? It looked terribly easy.'

'Did it?' He grinned. No further comment.

'You couldn't?'

'No, love, I could not. What's more I wouldn't, even if I could. It's obviously the will of Allah that you should go back to Dar Ibrahim, and for once the will of Allah is perfectly timed. By which I mean that it coincides with mine. You're going back – and I'm coming with you.'

'You are? You mean you're going to show John Lethman that letter now, and get him to let you in?'

'No. John Lethman has nothing to do with it. You're going to let me in yourself.'

I sat up abruptly. 'If you mean what I think you mean—'

'Probably. There's a back door, a postern.'

'So?' I asked sharply.

'I've been thinking . . .' He spoke slowly, his eyes still on the distant sprawl of the palace. 'The place where we met this morning, the ford . . . that was out of sight of the palace?'

'Yes. But Charles—'

'And you said that when you first saw me coming down the slope below the village, you thought I was your driver?'

'Yes, but Charles—'

'Now, they've seen your driver, but they've never seen me, and anyway they wouldn't be expecting me any more than you were. If they were looking out at all this morning, all they would see was you going down to the stream to meet your driver, who was walking down from the village. Fair enough?'

'Yes, but Charles, you can't! Are you really thinking—?'

'Of course I am. Now shut up and listen. I want to get into this place for myself and see exactly what's going on, and I want to get in now, not wait on Lethman's problematic good will. All right, it looks as if this flooding of the river has provided a heaven-sent chance; the will of Allah, plain and clear. Your part of it's perfectly simple and straightforward. You go back there now to the palace, ring for old Jassim again, and tell him what's more or less the truth. Tell him you couldn't cross the stream, and neither could your driver, but that you both went up the Nahr el-Sal'q as far as you could, to see if there was a place to cross. You got right up to the source, and there wasn't any place you could cross, even with the driver's help.' He grinned. 'Couldn't be truer so far. So you told your driver to go back to Beirut, and call for you again tomorrow when the stream had had a chance to go down. You also gave your driver a message for your cousin Charles, to say you were staying here another night, and that you'd join him tomorrow at the Phoenicia.'

'But, Charles—'

'They can hardly refuse to take you in. In fact, it sounded to me as if your Mr. Lethman was quite glad of your company. Who could blame him? If you had to live in a place like that you'd welcome the Abominable Snowman.'

'Thank you.'

'You're welcome. So, you get back into the palace. You told me they said you could explore anywhere you liked except the Prince's rooms. Well, do just that. You'll have hours of day-light this time. See if you can find this back door; you said it went from your end of the palace anyway.'

'It must do. I told you about the man walking

through the Seraglio Garden last night. Whoever it was, I'll swear he didn't come past my room to the main door, so he must have got in and out another way. But – you're serious? You're really planning to break in?'

'Why not? If you can find the door, see it's unlocked after dark tonight, and Mohammed will come to the mountain.'

'And if I can't find it?'

'Then we'll have to think of some other way. No windows at all looking back on the plateau – no, I can see that from here; there aren't. Well, but you said there was an arcade of sorts on the north side facing the village, and a path underneath?'

'There is, but the windows are all barred. Don't forget it was a harem.'

'You said the place was falling to bits; aren't any of the grilles broken? Or could they be broken?'

'Yes, I think so. But they're right up high in the wall, and—'

'Well, I can climb,' said Charles. 'If the wall's in bad repair there'll be plenty of footholds. I've always wanted to climb into a harem.'

'I'll bet. But why not try the direct approach first? With me, I mean, at the main gate?'

'Because if it doesn't work you mightn't get in either, and then there'd be no chance even of a break-in. And I'd sooner by-pass Lethman in any case.'

I started to ask why, saw my cousin's face, and decided to save time and energy. I know Charles. I asked instead: 'Well, once you're in, what then? What if you're caught?'

'All that'll happen is a bit of a row, or at worst a turn-up with John Lethman, and I'll risk that. It won't worry me, and at least I'll get to see Aunt H, if only to have her tear a strip off me.'

I regarded him. 'This I just don't get. I mean, curiosity is one thing, but this sudden outburst of devotion . . . No, Charles, it simply isn't on. It's all very fine and large, but you just can't do this sort of thing.'

'Can't I? Look at it this way. You've got to go back tonight. You don't want to. Wouldn't you rather I was there too?'

'Under the circumstances,' I said, 'I'd be glad of the Abominable Snowman.'

'Thank you. Well then, sweet Christabel—'

Of course I protested further, and of course he won in the end, as he always had. Besides, his last argument was the most cogent of the lot. However 'romantic' my last night at Dar Ibrahim had been, I had no desire to repeat it alone.

'Then that's settled.' He got decisively to his feet. 'I'll climb back across now, and in due course, if they're interested, they'll see me going back towards the village. Now, you said you'd finished supper by about ten, and Aunt H didn't send for you until about twelve. Just in case she decides to receive you again, we'd better say that I'll be at the back of the place any time from ten-thirty on. If you can't get the postern un-locked, I'll give a couple of barks like a hill fox under the wall, and if it's all clear for me to climb up, hang a towel out, or something light-coloured that I can see. Soap-opera stuff, I know, but simple ideas usually work out best. In fact, if it's climbable, I'd prefer the window, if the hounds get the run of the place at night.'

'Lord, yes, I'd forgotten that . . . I don't know if I could do anything about them. If he does take me up to see Aunt H again, there's a chance he may shut them up, but otherwise—'

'Have to chance it, don't worry. It's a big place. Let's get back, shall we?'

'What about the faun?'

'I dare say I could buy his silence, wouldn't you say?'

'I'm darned sure you could,' I said.

'And there's no one in the village going to be able to cross the Narh el-Sal'q to report that a white Porsche has been standing in the village street all day. Incidentally, I'll wait for a bit till I've made sure they've let you back into the palace. If they don't, come down again to the ford, and we'll think again. But I'm certain they will.'

'It's all very well for you. I don't want to have to spend another night without even a nightie.'

'That's not my fault, that's the will of Allah. I'll bring you a toothbrush tonight, but I'm damned if I'll climb back across the cascade carrying a nightie. You could always borrow a *djibbah* from Great-Aunt Harriet.'

And on this note of unfeeling comfort he led the way back towards the cascade and the gully.

8

But who shall teach thee what the night-
comer is?

The Koran: Sura LXXXVI

IT all went exactly as Charles would have wished. It
seemed almost too easy. Jassim may have imagined it
was Nasirulla who was ringing for entry, for he opened
the gate immediately, and when he saw who it was,
let me in with not much more than a bit of sulky
muttering, and in a moment or two I was explaining the
circumstances to John Lethman.

If he was put out he concealed it very well. 'How
stupid of me not to have expected this, especially when
Nasirulla didn't turn up. It's happened before after
heavy rain when the snows are still melting. Of course
you must stay. Did you really go the whole way up the
river to try and find a way across?'

'Yes, right up to the source, at least I suppose it's the
source, it's a sort of cascade coming out of the cliff.
The driver thought there might be a way over if he
helped me, but it would have taken a rock-climber, and
I jolly well wasn't going to risk it. So he gave up, and I
came back.'

'He's gone back to Beirut?'

I nodded. 'He said there'd be no chance of its going down before tomorrow. So I gave him a message for my cousin Charles not to come up here, because Great-Aunt Harriet wasn't well enough to see him.' I added: 'That's how I put it, anyway. I'll explain better when I see him myself. Are you going to tell her I've come back?'

He hesitated, then turned up a hand, smiling. 'I'm not sure. Let's defer the decision until she wakes up, shall we?'

'You play by ear, do you?'

'Exactly that. Come back to your garden, Miss Mansel. You're just in time for lunch.'

Whether Jassim had managed to convey the news to Halide, or whether she would normally have shared the meal with John Lethman herself, I had no way of telling. Only a few minutes after he had shown me back to the room in the Seraglio Court, the girl arrived with a tray set for two, which she thumped down with patent resentment on the table, and then stood smouldering at me and directing a rapid stream of Arabic at John Lethman which sounded like nothing more nor less than the spitting of an angry cat.

He took it calmly, only once interrupting with slight irritation, and finally, with a glance at his watch, making some statement that seemed to satisfy her. At any rate it silenced her and sent her away, with another look at me and a flouncing swirl of black skirts. No pretty silks this morning, I noticed, and no paint; just a working dress of rusty black, and none too clean at that. I thought with half-irritated amusement that if it was competition she was worrying about, she need hardly count me; I hadn't seen hot water or a hairbrush for more than twenty-four hours, and must look the worse for my long, hot trek up the Nahr el-Sal'q and back; but it wasn't exactly possible to explain that I wasn't entering the competition anyway.

Lethman was looking embarrassed. 'I'm sorry about that. Have a drink.'

He brought a glass of wine and handed it to me. As I took it our hands touched. His was reddish-brown, mine pale brown; but both what you would call white. Perhaps she had reason after all.

'Poor Halide,' I said, and sipped the wine. It was the same cool golden stuff of yesterday. I added quickly: 'It isn't fair when she has so much to do. Would she be offended if I left her something? I didn't this morning because I wasn't quite sure.'

'Offended?' There was the slightest edge on his voice. 'You can't offend an Arab with money.'

'How very sensible,' I said, and helped myself from a dish of *kefta*, savoury meat balls on a mound of rice. 'This waterfall I saw at the top of the Narh el-Sal'q, does it have any part in the Adonis cult you were telling me about?'

'Not really, though there's a minor site near by which was supposed to be a subsidiary of the temple of Venus at Afka. You wouldn't see it unless you climbed up out of the gorge . . . no? Well, it's hardly worth a special trip . . .'

The rest of the luncheon passed pleasantly, and it

was easy enough to keep him on impersonal subjects. This much to my relief. I didn't want to strain my talent for deception too far, and my recent meeting with Charles was just a little too vivid in my mind. Any further discussion of family affairs was better avoided, and I wasn't anxious to press for another interview with Great-Aunt Harriet. And here it seemed probable that John Lethman's interests coincided with my own.

As soon as lunch was over he got to his feet. If I didn't mind . . . ? He had things he must see to . . . If I would excuse him now . . . ? I reassured him quickly, almost too eagerly. The garden was drowsy with the afternoon's heat, and I would sit there, I told him, and doze over a book. And if I might do a bit of exploring later on? Not the Prince's Court, of course, but else-where? So fascinating . . . a chance I might never have again . . . and of course I wouldn't dream of disturbing Great-Aunt Harriet . . . no earthly need for her even to *know* . . . .

We parted on a mutual note of restrained relief. After he had gone, taking the tray with him, I collected some cushions off the window-seat and took them out into the garden, where I settled myself at the edge of the pool in the shade of a tamarisk tree.

It was very quiet. The trees hung still, the water was a flat, flashing glass, the flowers drooped in the heat. Near me on the stone a lizard slept motionless, not even moving when a quail shuffled past to settle in the dust, wings outspread. On the broken bridge the peacock displayed half-heartedly to a mate who wasn't even watching. Somewhere among the blazing magenta flowers of the bougainvillaea which covered the arcade a bird sang, and I recognised last night's king, the nightingale. Somehow, he didn't sound the same as he had with the trappings of storm and starlight. Some finches and a turtle-dove started up in opposition, and the nightingale, with a trill that sounded like a yawn, gave up. I didn't blame him. I slept.

It was about an hour later that I woke, and the sleepy heat seemed to have overtaken the whole place. Now, there was no sound at all. When I got up from my cushions the lizard flicked out of sight, but the quail never moved its head from under its wing. I set out to explore.

There is little point in describing here in detail my wanderings of that afternoon. It wasn't likely that any outer gate would open straight into the women's quarters, but the 'postern' had been at the back, and since the Seraglio Court, with its rooms and enormous garden, stretched the full width of the palace at the rear, my search had obviously to start there. Now, the postern had apparently been hidden in the trees at the south-eastern corner. When I looked out of my bedroom window I could just see the tops of those trees where they projected beyond the corner. They were level with my window-sill. The Seraglio, was in fact, a storey and a half above the level of the plateau. The postern must open on some corridor below it, or at the foot of a flight of steps.

A hunt along the eastern arcade and into the recesses of the hammam on the corner convinced me that there was no staircase there, nor a door that could lead to one, so after a while I abandoned the Seraglio, and set out to investigate the untidy sprawl of the palace buildings.

I am sure that the place was not as vast as I imagined it to be, but there were so many twisting stairs, narrow, dark corridors, small rooms opening apparently haphazard, one out of the other – many of them in half darkness and all untidy with the clutter and decay of years – that I very soon lost all sense of direction, and simply wandered at random. Every time I came to a window I looked through it to get my bearings, but many of the rooms were lit only by skylights, or by narrow windows giving on corridors. Here and there a window would look over the countryside; one small court, indeed, had an open arcade giving straight out over the Adonis gorge, with a magnificent view of snow-clad peaks beyond, and a sheer drop to the river below. One ground-floor window, I remember, looked north from the end of a black corridor, towards the village; but this window was barred, and beside it were two heavy doors with grills inset, giving on what I had no difficulty in recognising as prison cells.

After wandering for nearly two hours, getting my hands grimy and my shoes grey with dust, I was no nearer finding any door that could be the postern, or any staircase that took me down to it. Certainly during my wanderings I had come across several locked doors. The most promising of these was on the east side of the *midan*, a high door with a barred ventilator. But when (the place being apparently deserted for the afternoon) I pulled myself up for a quick glance through, I could see nothing except a yard or two of roughly cobbled flooring leading into darkness, apparently on the level and in the wrong direction. No sign of stairs – and in any case the door was fast locked. There were, of course, stairways in plenty that led crazily and seemingly at random from one level to another, but I found nothing that could definitely be called a basement or lower storey. The longest flight of steps counted only twelve, and led up to a gallery surrounding some echoing chamber big enough for a ballroom, where swallows nested in the roof, and the bougainvillaea had come in through the unglazed window arches. These running along the gallery at knee height, lighted the two long sides of the chamber, one row looking out to the south, the other inwards over an otherwise unlighted corridor. Hot buttresses of sunlight thrust diagonally in through the outer arches: round them the magenta flowers hung limp and still; the sound of the water from the gorge below came as little more than a murmur.

Quarter to five. I moved to the shady inner side of the gallery and sat down rather wearily on a deep sill to rest. Either the 'postern' was a mirage after all, or it was irrevocably hidden from me by one of the locked doors. My search could not have been anything but perfunctory, but I dared not take it further. The chance simply hadn't come off. Charles would have to climb in after all. And (I thought irritably, brushing dust from my slacks) serve him right.

In one respect my luck had been in; I had met no one all afternoon, though under the complex of watching windows I had been careful to preserve the air of an innocent and random explorer. I did wonder several times if the hounds were loose, and if the fact that they had seen me in John Lethman's company would make them friendly; but I need not have worried, I saw nothing of them. If they were still shut in the small court, they made no sign. Doubtless they, too, slept in the heat of the afternoon.

I was roused by the sound of a door opening somewhere below me on the far side of the corridor. The siesta was over, the place was waking up. I had better get back to my room in case someone thought of bringing tea.

Light steps on stone, and the gleam of scarlet silk. Halide paused in the doorway, looking back to speak softly to someone still in the room, her slim brown hands languidly adjusting the gilded belt at her waist. She had discarded her working-clothes; this time the dress was scarlet over pale green, and her gilt sandals had high heels and curved Persian toes. The bird had its plumage on again, and prettier than ever.

Mating plumage, at that. It was John Lethman's voice that answered her from the room, and a moment later he followed her to the door. He was wearing a long Arab robe of white silk, open to the waist, and his feet were bare. He looked as if he had just woken up.

It was too late to move now without being seen: I kept still.

The girl said something more, and laughed, and he pulled her towards him, still half sleepily, and made some reply against her hair.

I edged back from the window, hoping they were too absorbed to catch the movement and look up. But almost immediately a sound, familiar by now but almost shocking in the drowsy silence, froze me to my window-sill. The bell from the Prince's Divan. And after it, inevitably, the clamour of the hounds.

I don't know what I had expected to happen then – some reaction from Halide, perhaps, like the fear she had shown last night; certainly a rush to answer that arrogant summons. But no such thing happened. The two of them raised their heads, but stayed where they were, Halide (I thought) looking slightly startled, and throwing a question at John Lethman. He answered shortly, and then she laughed. A stream of Arabic from her, punctuated by laughter, then he was laughing too, and the hounds stopped their noise and fell quiet. Then the man pushed the girl away from him, with a gesture and a jerk of the head which obviously meant 'You'd better go', and, still laughing, she put a hand up to push the tumbled hair back from his brow, kissed him, and went, not hurrying.

I made no attempt to move. I stayed where I was, staring after her. And for the first time since Charles had made his fantastic proposal for tonight's break-in, I was whole-heartedly glad of it. I could hardly wait to tell him what I had seen.

Halide had been wearing Great-Aunt Harriet's ruby ring.

There was no mistake about it. As she had lifted her hand to John Lethman's hair, the light, falling from some source in the room behind him, had lit the jewel unmistakably. And she had laughed when the bell had rung, and gone, but not hurrying.

I stared after her, chewing my lip. I had a sudden picture of the lamplit room last night; the old woman wrapped up, huddled in the welter of wool and silk on her bed in the corner; Halide beside her, watching all the time with that wary look; and behind me John Lethman . . .

He went back into the room and shut the door.

I gave it three minutes, then went quietly downstairs from the gallery, and made my way back to the Seraglio Court.

At first I thought that Charles's alternative plan – the 'soap-opera' one – was also doomed to failure. In the last brief hour between daylight and darkness – between six and seven o'clock – I explored the arcade on the north side of the lake. Still carefully looking as if I was interested only in the view outside, I wandered from window to window examining the metal grilles and the state of the stone that held them. All were sound enough – too sound for me to be able to do anything about it, and the only one that wasn't barred had been boarded up with heavy shutters. Here and there, it is true, a bar was broken or bent, or the edge of the grille had rusted out of the rotten stone; but the grille was in heavy six-inch squares, and only a gap of half the window would have served to let a body through. There was no such gap, nothing that would have let anything in larger than a cat or a small and agile dog.

And if there had been, I thought bitterly, surprised at my own furious disappointment, it would have been blocked up somehow. Charles and I had been too sanguine. This was after all a lonely place, and Great-Aunt Harriet had the reputation of being rich. It was only reasonable, whatever the interior of the building was like, that the guards on the only accessible windows should be kept in good repair.

I am ashamed to say that I had stood there for a full five minutes staring at the barred windows and wondering what in the world to do next, before the thought hit me with all the beautiful simplicity and force of the apple dropping on Newton's head. One of the windows *had* been blocked. The end one. By a shutter.

And a shutter that was put up from inside could presumably be taken down from inside.

I ran along the arcade and peered anxiously at it in the now fading light.

At first sight it looked horribly permanent. Stout wooden shutters with nails as big as rivets were closed tightly over from either side like double doors, and across these a heavy bar, or rather plank, was nailed to hold them together. But when I examined this more closely, fingering the nails that held it in place. I found to my joy that they were not nails, but screws, two to each end, big-headed screws that I thought I might be able to manage. Surely among the assorted junk that I had seen lying around, there would be something that would do the job?

I didn't have far to look; most of the rooms were empty, some even open to the air with doors broken or left standing wide; but three doors down from the corner I remembered a room that – when I had literally pushed my way in to find a way to the postern – had looked like an abandoned junk-shop.

It had been at some time a bedroom, but would have a rated a poor fourth class in the tattiest hotel guide, The sagging bed, the broken table, every inch of the dusty floor was covered with a clutter of the most useless looking objects. I picked my way over a camel saddle, an old sewing-machine and a couple of swords, to a chest of drawers where I remembered seeing, beside a pile of dusty books, a paper-knife,

It was good and heavy and should do the job admirably. I carried it to the door and blew the dust off, to find it was no paper-knife at all, but a quite genuine dagger, an affair with an elaborately inlaid handle and a workmanlike steel blade, I ran back to the shuttered window.

The screw I tackled first was rusty and had bitten deeply into the wood, so after a few minutes' struggle I abandoned it and attacked the other one. This, though stiff at first, came out eventually. I went to the other end. The bar was lying on a slant, and I had to stand on tiptoe to deal with the other two screws, but after some difficulty got one of them out, and the other moving fairly easily. I left it there. There was no point in opening the shutters yet, before John Lethman had been and gone. I didn't bother with the rusted screw; if I freed one end of the bar I could pull it down using the rusted screw as a hinge, and leave it hanging there.

No one was likely to miss the dagger. I hid it under

the cushions of the window-seat in my room, went along to the hammam to wash, and regained my room just in time to meet Jassim carrying a lighted lamp, a bottle of arak, and a note from John Lethman to say that he himself had to dine with Great-Aunt Harriet, but food would be brought to me at nine and he would come along at ten to make sure I had everything I wanted for the night.

The note concluded: 'I didn't tell her you'd come back. It didn't seem quite the time. I'm sure you'll understand.'

I thought I understood very well. I put the note into my handbag, and regarded the bottle of arak with loathing, I'd have given an awful lot for a nice cup of tea.

He came as he had promised, staying chatting for half an hour, and went shortly after ten-thirty taking my supper tray with him. At something just after eleven I heard again the furious peal of Great-Aunt Harriet's bell, and somewhere in the palace the sound of a slamming door. Thereafter, silence. I turned out my lamp, sat for a little while to let my eyes get used to the darkness, then opened the door of my room and went out into the garden.

The night was warm and scented, the sky black, with that clear blackness that one imagines in outer space. Hanging in it, the clustered stars seemed as large as dog-daisies, and there was a crescent moon. Here and there its light struck a gleam from the surface of the lake. A couple of nightingales sang one against the other in a sort of wild angelic counterpoint, punctuated from the water with rude noises from the frogs. In the shadow of a pillar I nearly fell over a sleeping peahen, which went blundering off with loud expostulations between the pillars, disturbing a covey of rock partridges which exploded in their turn, grumbling, through the bushes. A few frogs dived with a noise like the popping of champagne corks.

Altogether it was a fairly public progress, and by the time I reached the shuttered window I was waiting, with every nerve jumping, for the hounds to add their warning to the rest. But they made no sign. I gave it a minute or two, then tackled the window.

The screw answered easily to the dagger, and I lowered the bar.

I had been afraid that the shutters might prove to be fixed in some way, but the right-hand one shifted when I pulled at it, and finally came open with a shriek of rusty hinges that seemed to fill the night. Recklessly I shoved it back to the wall and waited, straining my ears. Nothing, not even from the nightingales, which had apparently been shocked into silence.

So much the better. I pulled the other side open and leaned out.

And I could lean out. I had been right about the reason for the shutters. Except for a few inches of crumbling iron sticking out of the stone here and there, the grille had gone completely. I hung over the sill and strained my eyes to see.

The window was about thirty feet from the ground, and directly below it ran the path which skirted the north wall of the palace. Beyond the path the rocky ground fell away in a gentle bank covered with bushes, scrubby trees, and a few thin poplars which clung to the edge of the drop to the Nahr el-Sal'q. Off to the left I could see the sizeable grove of sycamores which shaded the top of the cliff path down to the ford.

Nothing of any height grew near, except the thin unclimbable poplars, and there were no creepers on the walls; but Charles, I thought, might be right, and the decaying state of the palace be in his favour. I couldn't see much in the moonlight, but here and there below me something furred or broke the line of the masonry, indicating that ferns and plants had thrust the mortar from between the stones, and the rock below that, though sheer, looked rough enough to provide holds for a clever climber.

Well, that was up to my cousin. I strained my eyes to see if I could see any movement, or even possibly the brief flash of a torch, but saw nothing. Beyond the near shapes of the trees all was darkness, a wide still darkness where blacker shapes loomed, but nothing was clear to the eye except the strung lights of the village and the distant glint of snows under the young moon. He would have had to make the climb across the top of the Nahr el-Sal'q by moon or torchlight, and even that climb was probably simple compared with this sheer wall below me, where he wouldn't dare use his torch at all. It occurred to me suddenly to wonder if there were a rope in the junk-room, or anywhere else in the court. If so, one of the projecting pieces of iron might be strong enough to hold it. I hung my white towel over the window-sill as a signal that the way was clear, and turned to hurry back along the arcade.

Something moved in the bushes near the end of the broken bridge. Not one of the peacocks; this was too big; and moved too purposefully. I stood still, my heart suddenly thumping. It forged through the crackling thicket, and a thousand scents came with it, as sharp as spice from the crushed leaves. Then it came slowly out on to the flagway in the moonlight, and stood staring at me. It was one of the hounds. Almost immediately I heard a splashing sound, followed by the swift scrabble of paws on stone, and the other came racing round the edge of the lake towards me.

I stayed where I was, frozen. I don't think it occurred to me straight away to be afraid of the dogs themselves; I assumed John Lethman to be with them, approaching through the garden. What was frightening me was the thought of the tell-tale window behind me, with my All Clear hanging in it inviting Charles to begin his climb . . .

The second dog had stopped beside the first, and the pair stood shoulder to shoulder, rigid, heads high and ears pricked. They looked very big, and very alert. They were between me and my bedroom. Charles or no Charles, I'd have given a lot at that moment to have heard John Lethman's tread and his voice calling them in.

But nothing moved – they must be patrolling on their own. I wondered fleetingly how they had got into the Seraglio; Lethman must have left the main door open when he went with my supper tray, and like a fool

I hadn't checked. Of course, if they did give tongue, Charles would hear them and be warned. Or if they attacked me, and I screamed for John Lethman . . .

The only thing to do was to stand perfectly still and stare back at them. The moonlight caught their eyes, reflecting back brilliantly. Their ears were cocked high, their long narrow heads making them look predatory, like foxes.

'Good dogs,' I said falsely, putting out a reluctant hand.

There was a horrible pause. Then one of them, the bigger of the two, gave a sudden little whine, and I saw the ears flatten. In a sort of dazed relief I realised that the plumed tail was stirring. The smaller hound seemed to take a cue from this. Her ears went back, her head down, and she crept forward towards me, wagging her tail.

Relief made me feel weak at the knees. I sat down on the edge of a stone tub containing tobacco flowers, and said, on a breathless gasp: 'Good dog, oh good *dog!* Here, chaps, here – and keep quiet for Pete's sake . . .' What the blazes were their names? Soupy? Soapy? Softy? Surely not . . . ! Sofi, that was it, and Star. 'Star!' I said, 'Sofi! Come on now – here – that's right . . . Keep quiet, you great dollops, you great soft idiots . . . Watchdogs my foot . . . ! Oh, you horrible dog, you're wet. . . .'

And the hounds were delighted. We made a rather confused, damp, and reasonably quiet fuss of one another, till I felt absolutely certain they were safe to handle, then I got to my feet, feeling for their collars, ready to put them out and clear the field for Charles.

'Come along now, chaps. You'd better get back on the job, you dangerous brutes, you. We've got a burglar coming any minute now, and I want you out of here.'

At that precise moment, from directly below the north wall, I heard Charles's signal, the sharp double bark of a hill fox.

The salukis, naturally, heard it too. Their heads went up, and I felt the bigger one – the dog – stiffen. But it must have sounded to them a fairly unconvincing fox – and a foreign one at that – for when I grabbed for their collars again, murmuring soothingly, they allowed me to pull them away towards the gate.

They were so tall that I didn't have to stoop, but hurried along the flagged path with a hand hooked in each collar. That is, I tried to hurry, but whatever sounds they were hearing from the far end of the garden so intrigued them that they hung heavily against their collars, looking back now and again with little whining noises deep in their throats, so that I expected at any moment the outcry to begin. But there was no outcry, and at length I got them to the gate – to find it, against all expectations, firmly shut.

No time to stop and wonder how on earth they had found their way in; there were probably a dozen decaying holes in the walls that they knew perfectly well. I concentrated on getting them shut out. It was a bit of a struggle to hold both dogs and get the door undone at the same time, but eventually I managed, and with a final pat pushed both hounds outside, shut the gate firmly on them, and dropped the latch into place.

For a moment all was stillness again. The sounds from the end of the garden had stopped, though, straining my eyes, I though I saw movement in the far shadows. A moment later I heard the soft footstep. He was in.

I had started to meet him, when to my horror I heard the dogs begin to whine and bark just outside the gate; the eager scrabbling of paws on wood as loud as a charge of galloping horses. They still sounded absurdly friendly – too damned friendly; it seemed that even the burglar from outside rated a noisy welcome on the mat. I could see him fairly clearly now, coming rapidly along in front of the pillars of the eastern arcade.

I ran to meet him. 'I'm sorry, but it's the dogs, the blasted dogs! They got in somehow and they're making a ghastly noise, and I don't know what to do with them!'

I stopped abruptly. The shadowy figure had come up to me.

'I'm fearfully sorry,' he said, 'did they frighten you? That idiot Jassim left a door open and they got through.'

The newcomer wasn't Charles at all. It was John Lethman.

9

Of my Base Metal may be filed a key,
That shall unlock the Door . . .
> E. FitzGerald: *The Rubáiyát*
> of Omar *Khayyám*

IT was probably a very good thing that the dark was
hiding my expression. There was a long, ghastly pause,
while I could think of nothing whatever to say. I did a
desperate mental recap of the way I had greeted him,
decided it couldn't have given much away or he
wouldn't have sounded so unsurprised, thanked Allah
I hadn't actually called him 'Charles' and settled on
attack as the best form of defence.

'How in the world did you get in?'

I thought he hesitated for a moment. Then I saw the
movement of his head. 'There's a door over in the far
corner. Hadn't you found it in your wanderings?'

'No. Was it open?'

'I'm afraid so. It's not a door we usually use at all, it
only gives on a warren of empty rooms between here
and the Prince's Court. Probably his suite and personal
slaves were kept there once.' He gave a short laugh. 'It
isn't even fit for the slaves now, nothing there but the

rats. That's probably why the dogs went ramping through – they're not allowed near the Prince's rooms normally, but Jassim must have left a door open somewhere. Did they frighten you?'

He was speaking softly, as I suppose one does instinctively in a quiet night. I was only half attending to what he said. I was wondering if the sounds I had heard before had in fact been sounds of Charles's climb, or only of John Lethman's approach. If the latter, had Charles heard him too, and waited at the foot of the wall, or was he likely to erupt at any minute from the window?

I raised my own voice to normal pitch. 'They did rather. Why in the world did you tell me they were savage? They're actually terribly friendly.'

He laughed again, a bit too easily. 'They can be sometimes. I see you managed to put them out, anyway.'

'They probably recognised me as one of the family – or else they saw me with you yesterday, so they know I'm allowed in. Are there only the two? Didn't she have some small dogs – pets?'

'She used to have a pack of spaniels, then some terriers. The last of them died just last month. You mightn't have got away with it if he'd still been around.' Again the abrupt laugh. ' "Pet" was hardly the word, really . . . Look, I really am terribly sorry about this. You weren't in bed, I take it?'

'No. I was just thinking of going. I'd just put the lamp out, and I came out to look at the garden. Can you smell the jasmine and tobacco flowers? And don't the roses ever go to sleep?' I moved determinedly towards the gate as I spoke, and he came with me. 'If it comes to that, don't you? Were you doing the rounds, or just trying to find the dogs?'

'Both. I was wondering whether you'd been counting on seeing your great-aunt again.'

'No. I wasn't staying up for that, honestly. I was just on my way to bed. Don't give it a thought, Mr Lethman, I quite understand. Good night.'

'Good night. And don't worry you'll be disturbed again, I've locked the other door, and I'll see this one's safe.'

'I'll lock it myself,' I promised.

The gate closed behind him. There were strangled yelps of welcome from the dogs, and then the sounds receded into the labyrinth of the palace. At least the disconcerting little interlude had given me a watertight excuse for locking the Seraglio gate on the inside. The key turned with a satisfying *clunk*, and I fled back towards the open window.

It was my night for shocks. I'd got two-thirds of the way back along the water-side when a soft 'Christy' brought me up short, and a shadow detached itself from a dark doorway, and materialised as my cousin.

I gasped, and turned on him furiously, and quite unjustly. 'You high-powered nit, you scared me silly! I thought – when did you get *in*?'

'Just before he did.'

'Oh, you saw him then?'

'I'll say. Lethman?'

'Yes. He got in by a door in the far corner. The dogs must have—'

'Like hell he did. He came from the island,' said Charles curtly.

'From the *island*? He couldn't have!'

'I tell you I saw him. I heard some queer noises when I was half way up the wall, so I went pretty cautiously, and took a quiet little gander over the still before I climbed in. I saw you and the dogs making off down the path. I left you get down to the far end, then I couldn't hang on much longer, so I heaved myself in through the window. Next thing was, I saw him coming across the bridge.'

'But – you're sure?'

'Are you joking? He went past within feet of me. I'm permanently crippled through jack-knifing down too near a prickly pear. After he'd gone by I went back into one of the rooms and hid.'

'But if he's been on the island all the time, he must have seen me open the window. Those shutters made the most awful noise. He must have guessed why I was opening them up, so why didn't he tackle me, or wait a bit longer to see what I was up to? Charles, I don't like it! It's all very well saying that even if you were caught there wouldn't be much trouble, but this is just the kind of place where they'd loose off a shotgun at you or something, on spec. *And why didn't he wait?* What's he gone to do?'

'Dear girl, don't get so steamed up. If he had seen you at the window he'd obviously have asked what the blazes you thought you were doing, and whatever guess he made, he'd have stopped you. So obviously he didn't see you. *Quod erat.*'

'I suppose so . . .' I added quickly: 'Now I come to think about it – yes, the dogs could have been on the island. I saw Star – that's the big one – by the bridge, and when Sofi came there was a lot of splashing, and she was wet. Perhaps John Lethman heard them over there and went across to get them . . . ? No, that won't do, because then he'd have seen me. But he'd have seen me too if he'd come by a door in the far corner. He'd have passed me when I was at the window. Oh, I give up! Charles, what on earth's it all about? Why should he lie?'

'I don't know. But when we know how, we know why. Is there really a door in the corner?'

'I don't know, I didn't see one. But it's terribly overgrown and I didn't really search, because it wasn't the right place for the postern.'

'Supposing we look, then? He got in somehow, didn't he, and not by the main door. And if he was on the island all the time, and didn't ask you what the blazes you were up to, I could bear to know why. Does the main door lock, by any chance?'

'I locked it.'

'And bonny sweet Christy was all my joy. What the sweet hell's that?'

'A peacock. Do be careful, Charles, they're all asleep.'

'With cat-like thump upon our way we steal. Can you see in the dark, love?'

'Just about, by this time,' I said. 'And incidentally, so

can John Lethman. You'd think if he was doing his rounds in this boneyard of a place he'd show a torch, wouldn't you? I suppose it didn't enter your head to bring one?'

'You wrong me every way; you wrong me, Brutus. But we'll do without as long as we can.'

'You're very high tonight, aren't you?'

'The intoxication of your presence. Besides, I'm enjoying myself.'

'As a matter of fact, so am I, now you're here.'

'Watch it,' said my cousin, 'there's a prickly pear on your near bumper.' He pulled back a bough for me, and dropped a casual arm round my shoulders to steer me through. He must have seen me smiling, for he asked:

'What is it? Penny for them.'

'Brotherly love.'

'Meaning me?'

'Well, you're the only bro. I've got.'

' "The near in blood the nearer bloody",' he quoted absently, peering ahead. 'There's your door, I think?'

'Where?'

He pointed. 'Under the luxuriant herb, whatever it is.'

'You ignorant peasant, that's jasmine. It's terribly dark here, could we use the torch? That's it . . . aha!'

'What d'you mean, aha?'

'Look,' I said.

Charles looked. He could hardly avoid seeing what I had meant. There was certainly a door, and it was certainly decayed, but nothing – neither dogs nor man

– had been through it for a very long time. The weeds grew a foot high in front of it, and the hinges looked like spindles of wool, so thickly were they cocooned with cobwebs.

'Aha, indeed,' said my cousin. 'And a beautiful web right across it, too, just in case we thought it might have been opened the other way. But how corny, no clichés spared . . . but then things only become clichés because they're the slickest way of saying something. No, this door hasn't been opened since the last time the old Emir tottered along to the harem in 1875. *Videlicet* – if that's the word I want, which seems doubtful – the spiders. So he didn't come in this way, our John Lethman. Well, I hardly thought so. Come back, come back, Horatius.'

I said blankly: 'But there *can't* be a way in from the island!'

'We can but look,' said Charles reasonably. 'Hullo!' The beam of the torch, narrow and bright and concentrated, speared down through the weeds at the foot of the wall, to light a tombstone, a small flat slab let into the masonry, and carrying a name deeply tooled: JAZID.

'A graveyard, no less,' said Charles, and sent the torchlight skidding along a couple of feet. Another stone, another legend: OMAR.

'For goodness' sake, turn it up!' I exclaimed. 'D'you mean it really is a graveyard? In here? But why on earth . . . ? And anyway, they're men's names. They can't be—'

I stopped. The light had caught another one: ERNIE.

'Charles—'

'So that's it. I remember Ernie quite well.'

I said, exasperated: 'Be serious, for goodness' sake! You know perfectly well that Great-Uncle Ernest—'

'No, no, the dog. He was one of the King Charles spaniels she had when she first came out here. Don't you remember Ernie? She always said he was called after Great-Uncle Ernest because he was absent over everything but meals.' He sounded pretty absent himself, as if he was thinking hard, but not about what he was saying. The torchlight moved on. 'It's the pets' graveyard, hadn't you guessed? NELL, MINETTE, JAMIE, still the spaniels . . . HAYDEE, LALOUK, those sound more Eastern . . . Ah, here she is. DELILAH Alas, poor Delilah. That's the lot.'

'They can't have got round to him yet.'

'Who?'

'Samson. John Lethman says he died last month. Look, must we spend the whole night in a dogs' graveyard? What are you looking for?'

The torchlight drifted along the wall, met nothing but a tangle of creepers and the ghostly pale faces of flowers. 'Nothing,' said Charles.

'Then let's get out of here.'

'I am coming, my own, my sweet.' He snapped the light out, and swung back an armful of stems to let me through. 'I suppose that's a nightingale singing its ducky little heart out up there? Damn these roses, my sweater must look like a yak's pelt by now.'

'What does it take to make you romantic?'

'I'll tell you some day. Can you manage this?'

'This' was the bridge. The faint moonlight reflecting

back from the water below made the broken gap clearly visible; it wasn't as far as I had thought, perhaps five feet. Charles jumped it first, light-footed, and more or less caught me as I jumped after him. And soon, with a hand in his, I was treading carefully off the bridge on to the rocky shore of the island.

This was very small, being nothing more than an artistically placed tumble of rocks, planted with bushes and shrubs long gone wild, but designed to lead the eye up to the grove of shade-trees (of a kind I didn't recognise) which overhung the kiosk. This, as I have said, was a small summer pavilion, a circular building with slender pillars supporting a gilded dome. The door was an open archway, and to the sides, between the pillars, fretted lattices of stone made fantastic patterns where the moonlight fell. Wide shallow steps led up from the shore, and a tumble of creepers hung half across the doorway, darkening the interior. My cousin let go my hand, pulled some of the tangle aside, and flashed his torch on. With a clap and flurry of wings two pigeons hurtled out over his head, making him duck and swear, then he led the way in.

The interior was empty except for a small hexagonal basin in the centre of the floor where there must once have been a fountain playing. A green fish, solid verdigris, gaped dry-mouthed over dead water which hardly reflected back the torchlight. On two sides the floor was bracketed with wide semicircular couches, cushionless and filthy with twigs and birds' dropping. The wall opposite the doorway was solid, and painted all over. Charles shone the torch on this.

The painting was done in the Persian, rather than the Arab style, for I could see trees with fruit and flowers, and figures seated under them clad in rich blue and green robes, and something that might have been a hunting leopard leaping after a gazelle on a golden ground. I supposed that in daylight, like everything else in the place, it would be faded and dirty, but in the fleeting rich yellow of the torchlight it looked enchantingly pretty.

The scene was in three panels, a triptych divided by painted tree-trunks, stiff and formal, following the line of the pillars that framed the section of wall. At one edge of the centre panel, all down the side of the trunk, a dark line showed.

'Here we go,' said Charles, approaching it.

'You mean it's a door?'

He made no reply. He was playing the light slowly over the picture his hand following the probing beam, sliding and patting over the surface of the wall. Then he gave a grunt of satisfaction. From the middle of a painted orange tree a section of the leaves seemed to detach themselves into his hand; the ringbolt of a door. He turned it and pulled. The painted panel opened on quiet, accustomed hinges, showing a gap of blackness behind.

I found my heart beating faster. A secret door can't fail to be exciting, and in this setting . . . 'Where can it possibly go?' Then, as he made a gesture of quiet, and jerked a thumb downwards, I said on a whisper that threatened to choke itself with sudden excitement: 'You can't mean an underground passage?'

'What else? You notice this wall's flat, but if we looked round the back of this place, in the grove, we'd find the outer wall followed the curve of the rest, and the building was circular. There's room in the segment for the head of the shaft.' He laughed at my expression. 'Not so very surprising; these old palaces had as many doors and passages and secret exits as they had wormholes – all the go in the good old days when you slept with armed guards round the bed and ate with a couple of slaves tasting for poison.' He added: 'This is the harem. The Emir would have his private stairway, one would think.'

'My God, it's all it needed! Now all we want's a magic carpet or a genie in a bottle.'

He grinned. 'Hope on, hope ever, we may get one yet.' The light played over the door. 'This must be how he got in, and the dogs. In that case it probably pushes open quite easily from the inside, but I don't trust it, and I don't want to be locked down there for ever like the Mistletoe Bough. Let's find something to wedge it open with, shall we?'

'Down there?' I asked in alarm. 'You're not going down?'

'Why not? Can you resist it?'

'Easily . . . No, actually, Charles dear, this is all very exciting, but we shouldn't. It feels all wrong.'

'That's just the setting. If this was the back stairs at home you'd think nothing of it. It's all this Arabian Nights' stuff that's getting you.'

'I suppose that's true. Can you see?' This as he shone the torchbeam into the gap and stepped over the sill.

'Perfectly. There's a steep flight of steps here, in good repair, and even reasonably clean.'

'I don't believe it,' I said, as I took his outstretched hand, and stepped carefully over the sill after him.

But it was true. From just inside the painted door the steps went steeply downwards, spiralling round a central column. This seemed to be richly carved, and on the curved outer wall there were more paintings, similar to the one on the door. Dimly I could see the trunks of trees, and green interlacing boughs, and a pale flower-dotted ground where a racing camel, curiously elongated by the curve of the wall, carried a mustachioed warrior waving a sabre, and a lady unconcernedly playing a zither. Fastened to this wall was a handrail of some blackened metal that could have been brass, held at intervals by elaborate lizards or small dragons which clung riveted to the stones. Certainly an important stair-case, a royal staircase, the Prince's own way to the women's quarters. It would be his regular and by no means secret way; merely his private stair, as richly decorated and attractive as his own apartments. The pavilion was in fact the top storey of a circular tower or stone shaft which was let down through the centre of the lake into the solid rock on which the garden had been built.

'Coming?' said Charles.

'No – no, wait—' I hung back against his hand. 'Haven't you realised – if this is the Seraglio stair from the Prince's rooms, that means Great-Aunt Harriet's, and she'll be wide awake, probably with John Lethman reading aloud to her out of the twenty-seventh Sura of the Koran.'

He stopped. 'You've got a point there. But it must go somewhere else as well.'

'Must it?'

'The dogs came this way. I doubt if they're allowed to roam the old lady's bedroom at night, so they must have got through from elsewhere. And what's more, doesn't it occur to you that this might be a way to the postern?'

'Of course! It was on a lower level But oughtn't we wait a bit? If we met someone . . .'

'I must admit I'd sooner not,' said Charles. 'You're right, we'd better leave it for a bit.' He followed me back into the pavilion, and behind him the painted door shut silently on a cushion of dead air. Back in the latticed moonlight it was comparatively easy to see the way. He switched off the torch. 'What time does she settle down?'

'I've no idea,' I said, 'but John Lethman'll probably be around for a bit yet. Are you going to try and see her when he's gone?'

'I don't think so. Unless it were urgent, I wouldn't do it this way. It'd be enough to frighten an elderly person into fits, bursting in on her in the middle of the night. No, if I see her at all it'll be the legit, way, daylight and front gate and one clear call for me. But you know, on what's happened up to now I'm damned if I'll clear quietly out without taking a good look around. Would you?'

'Probably not. Anyway, if I've got to spend the rest

of the night here I'd rather you spent it with me than not.'

'Such passion,' said my cousin tranquilly. We were at the bridge now, and he paused and cocked his head to listen. Stillness held the place. No shadow moved. He started softly across the bridge, and I followed him.

'You're not going out of this court?' I whispered quickly. 'The dogs'll make an awful row—'

'No. I'm not interested in the part of the palace they let you loose in, only the part they didn't. The gap looks wider from this side, doesn't it? Think you can jump it if I catch you?'

'I can try. Charles, you said "they"? Are you making a bit of mystery out of all this? There's really no reason to suppose—'

'Probably not. I'm probably wrong anyway, Tell you later, alligator. Now jump.' I jumped, slipped on landing, and was caught and held. Ridiculous that I hadn't realised until this minute how strong he was. We climbed down off the bridge and pushed our way through the rustling bushes.

He said over his shoulder: 'Just in case we don't find the postern down there, we'll go now and take a look at my other line of retreat, shall we? I saw a rope in that room full of junk along here – at least I think I did. It would make life easier on the downward trail.'

'I thought there might be one there. I was just on my way to look when the dogs caught me. Do you suppose John Lethman got in via the island last night, too?'

'You can bet your boots he did,' said Charles shortly.

'But why not say so? Why lie? Did it matter?'

'Only if he wanted to stop you knowing there was a way under the lake.'

'You mean he was afraid I'd by-pass him and go straight to Aunt H on my own?'

'Possibly. But it seems a lot of trouble to go to for something that wouldn't have mattered very much, wouldn't you say?'

'I suppose so. And after all, I might have found it by myself. He didn't stop me wandering around exploring in here.'

We had gained the flagged pathway. After the darkness of the pavilion and the overhanging bushes, it seemed light here. Something shuffled rustling into the undergrowth, clucking to itself. I saw Charles slant a look at me. 'Why didn't you go over to the island before? I'd have thought that'd be the first thing. It's dead romantic.'

'I meant to, but when I got to the bridge . . .' I paused. 'Yes, I see, you mean that's what he counted on? I probably could have got across the broken bridge by myself, but it didn't seem worth the bother.'

'There you are. Unless you were wild keen, which you'd no particular reason to be, he could reckon you wouldn't be likely to bother, and even if you had jumped over you'd probably never have realised the painted wall was a doorway.'

'But if it was all that important that I shouldn't find the staircase, why put me in this court at all? I know it's probably the only reasonable bedroom, but if it *mattered*—'

'Simply because it is the Seraglio, and was designed as a sort of five-star gaol. There's probably a million ways in and out of every other corner of the palace, so he had to put you here and spin you the story about the savage dogs to keep you in. What's more,' he added, not sounding worried about it at all, 'we'll almost certainly find there's another door at the foot of the spiral stairway – the one Jassim left open for the dogs – and it'll equally certainly be locked now.'

I glanced at him, but he hadn't got the torch on, and I couldn't see his face. 'And if we do?'

'Well . . .' said my cousin, and left it at that.

I asked sharply: 'You don't mean that you could pick the lock?'

He laughed. 'That's the first note of honest admiration I've heard from you since the time I blew the apple-loft door open with carbide. Christy, my sweet, you were born to be a banker's moll. Take it from me, lock-picking is practically required study in Mansels.'

'Well, naturally. But—' I paused, then went on slowly: 'What this amounts to is that there really is something wrong going on . . . I haven't had time to tell you yet, but this afternoon I saw Halide wearing Great-Aunt Harriet's ruby ring – you remember the one? – and she and John Lethman are certainly having an affair, and not paying very much attention to Aunt H, either, from the look of things – which seemed odd, after last night, when they were so attentive in front of me.'

I told him then, very quickly, about the little scene I had glimpsed this afternoon. He had stopped to listen,

and against the moonlight I could see the attentive slant
of his head, but when I had finished he made no
comment, merely moving on along the arcade.

I followed. 'And why did he lie to me?' I persisted.
'There must be some reason for the lies about the way
he got in, and the hounds, too . . . Oh, he passed it off
tonight, but he really did make a lot of it before, how
savage they were, and how unsafe it would be for me to
wander about. He made rather a thing about their
being loose at night.'

'Probably wanted you contained in your own court
while he carried on his affair with the girl.'

'Come off it,' I said curtly. 'He was carrying that on
with me wandering about the place all afternoon.
Anyway, the palace is big enough, heaven knows.
Charles, she really was wearing that ring, and if you
ask me—'

'Hush a minute, I want to put the light on. Can you
hear anything?'

'No.'

'Then stay out here and keep your ears open while I
go in and look for a rope.'

He vanished through the doorway of the junk-room.

I looked after him thoughtfully. I might not have
seen him for four years, but I still knew every tone of
his voice as well as I knew my own. For some reason he
had suddenly clammed up on me. There was something he knew, or something he thought, that he didn't
propose to share with me. He had been stalling very
well, but still he had been stalling.

'Ah,' he said, from inside the room.

'Found one?'

'Not so long as a cur's tail, nor so strong as a cobweb, but 'twill serve. Hold the torch while I test it, will you . . . ? Good grief, it's filthy . . . Well, I wouldn't exactly climb the west face of the Dru with it, but it should help me down the wall if we don't find the back door.'

He emerged from the room, wiping the dirt off his hands. 'And now a wash, and a wait. We'll give it an hour, shall we? As long as I can get out of here and away by first light . . . It's even possible the Nahr el-Sal'q may have gone down dramatically by morning, and I can save myself a lot of trouble by cutting straight across it and away before anyone sees me.'

'Where's your car this time?'

'I left it about half a mile below the village. There's a small quarry where I could get it off the road and pretty well out of sight. I did play with the idea of spending the rest of the night in the car and coming across for you myself in the morning, but there's always the risk that someone might see it standing there in the small hours and Nasirulla bring the news over before you're clear of the place. And if I ever do want to see Aunt H, I don't fancy having to talk my way out of that one . . . So I left a message for Hamid to come up for you at half past nine tomorrow, and I'll go down to Beirut and wait for you there. And now show me your bathroom, Christy mine, and we'll listen to the nightingales while I get my picklocks sorted out.'

10

O softly tread, said Christabel.

S. T. Coleridge: *Christabel*

BUT they weren't needed after all.

When we set out again the thin moon had drifted higher, clear of the island trees, and by her faint light we negotiated the bridge once more, and made our way up into the pavilion. The painted door swung out silently, and Charles wedged it open with a stone. Torchlight speared ahead of us into the black gap as we stepped delicately inside and started down the spiral stair.

The paintings slid past us, spectral in the moving light. Domes and minarets, cypresses like spear-heads, gazelles, hawks, Arabian stallions, fruit-trees and singing-birds . . . and at the bottom a door.

Shut, of course. It looked massive and impassable in that frail light, but to my surprise, when Charles put a hand to it and pulled cautiously, it came easily, and with the same well oiled silence as the one above. I saw then that the latch was gone, and where the original lock had been was a splintered panel of wood. Part of the palace's history, no doubt, that smashed lock . . .

The door had been secured again in more recent times – and by a stout hasp and staple and a padlock – but a lock is only as strong as its moorings, and these, like the rest of the palace appointments, were rotten. The padlock was still in place, and locked, but on one side the hasp had been pulled away from the crumbling jamb, and hung there with one socket still holding the useless screw, the other empty.

This, then, was how the dogs had got through. It seemed probable that they had broken the lock themselves, and tonight, since otherwise it would surely have been mended again. And the damage was obviously recent, for splinters and sawdust showed on the floor, and when Charles shone the torch down I caught the gleam of the fallen screw.

'Luck,' he said softly.

'Good for the Gabriel Hounds,' I breathed.

He smiled, and beckoned. I soft-shoed after him through the door.

It was very dark, a great arched passage with ribbed and vaulted ceiling where the torchlight seemed little more than an impertinent gleam. We were at the end of a sort of underground T-junction, under a vault made by crossed arches. Our door closed one end of the top shaft of the T. A few yards along from us on the left, an open archway led off into blackness, some sort of passageway down which came a draught of air. Straight ahead, and closing the top bar of the T, was another door. Like the main gate of the palace, this door was of bronze, its panels elaborately worked and its surface – in spite of age and damage – retaining the silky beauty of hand-hammered metal. To either side of it were ornate iron brackets which must once have held torches, and beneath these we saw recesses in the wall, man-high like sentry boxes. The archway itself was carved, and held traces of peeling paint.

'Must be the Prince's door,' I whispered. 'You were right, it's the low road to the Seraglio. See if it's locked.'

But he shook his head and sent the light shifting from the door towards the passageway on the left.

'Line of retreat first,' he said softly. 'This way to the postern, what do you bet? Shall we go see?'

The tunnel was long and curved, not quite level, and very dark. Our progress was slow. As far as I could see the walls were of rough stone – no paintings here – and at intervals bore rusty iron brackets for lights. The floor was rough, too, big slabs of paving with a border of crude cobbles, all worn, filthy, and treacherous with holes. Once a scuffle in the blackness made me stop and clutch at Charles's arm, but the rat or whatever it was made off without my seeing it. The passage bent to the left, turned uphill a little, and met another at right angles.

We paused at the junction. Our passage was the main stem of another T, this time with a bigger passage crossing the head of it. Charles put the torch out, and we stood for a moment listening. The air was fresher here, and it was an easy guess that this corridor was open to the upper air. Then from somewhere away to the right I heard, faintly, the snuffle and whine of the hounds.

Charles flashed the light that way momentarily, to

show the rough floor of the tunnel mounting in wide and very shallow steps. 'That probably goes up to the gate you saw in the *midan*, which means, unless I'm wrong—' He turned the beam to the left, and almost immediately it seemed to focus on something lying in the middle of the sloping way. A scattered trail of droppings, horse or mule. 'I'm not wrong,' he said. 'This way.'

A minute or two later we were looking out through the grove of trees at the edge of the Adonis gorge.

The postern gate was built into the solid rock, recessed deeply into it, and below the level of the plateau behind the palace. A steep ramp cut from the rock led down to it through the grove, and the roots of the sycamores, level with the lintel, reached bare and twisted like mangroves half across the top of the doorway. A buttress protected it on the landward side, and weeds and creepers grew profusely among the tree roots and overhung the cutting from above. Anyone approaching from the plateau would have seen merely a buttress jutting out into the grove, and beyond this the drop to the Adonis gorge. The ramp was just wide enough for a laden beast, and the gate was a heavy, studded affair in excellent repair, both locked and barred.

'You see?' said my cousin. 'Just big enough to take a mule or horse – an emergency door – and the long passage leading under the Seraglio and up to the *midan*. Well this'll save me a climb, praise be to Allah. Nice of them to leave the key in the lock, wasn't it? Come back in – no, don't shoot the bolts again, I think we'll leave it unlocked.' Inside the shut gate again he glanced at his watch. 'After two. They can't stay up all night surely?'

'If anyone's still awake, it'll only be Aunt Harriet.'

'Yes,' said my cousin. 'Well . . .'

He was looking at the ground, fiddling with the button of the flashlight. As it came on again, I caught his expression. This was abstracted, even bleak. He glanced up suddenly. 'Shall we go back now?'

'Back? To the Prince's door? That'll be locked, too, I expect.' There must have been something in the ancient secrecies of the place that were making themselves felt; I found myself almost speaking with relief, and I saw him give me another quick glance.

'Possibly, though I doubt if they'd have the place sealed up internally, so to speak. Christy—'

'Yes?'

'Do you want to go on?'

'On?' We had reached the first T-fork and turned into the home run. 'Back here, you mean? Where else can we go?'

'I mean on to the Prince's door. Would you rather just go back to the Seraglio?'

'Would you?'

'No, not now. But if you'd rather get out from under and leave it to me—'

'Do me a favour, will you? I'm not afraid of John Lethman, even if you are.'

He started to say something, apparently thought better of it, then grinned and said merely: '*En avant, mes braves.*' We went on.

And the Prince's door wasn't locked. It opened silently, and beyond it was a long, vaulted corridor, pitch black and very still and quite empty. Charles paused. The torchlight seemed almost to be lost in the blackness ahead of us. I thought he hesitated a moment, then he went forward. I followed.

The corridor, like the spiral stair, had once been richly decorated, but though it was swept and reasonably clean underfoot it was in bad repair, and the painted landscapes on the walls were faded and peeling, and even in the torchlight could be seen to be very dirty. The floor was of marble, overlaid with some drab and tattered matting, on which our footsteps made no sound. The air was still and dead and smelled of dust.

To either side, at intervals, were doorways of the kind familiar to me from my wanderings in the palace, most of them gaps of darkness where broken doors hung open on emptiness or confusion. Charles shone the light into the first of these, which seemed to contain nothing but large earthenware jars.

'Nothing there but forty thieves,' he commented.

'What did you expect?'

'Heaven knows . . . And here's Aladdin's cave. Half a minute, let's look.'

At first I couldn't see what had caught his attention. The room seemed to contain much the same jumble as the 'junk-room' in the Seraglio; furniture, ornaments, cobwebs – the same dreary and neglected clutter of years. On a rickety chest of drawers was a pile of books, rather less dusty than the rest.

The torchlight probed along the pile, and after it went

Charles's fastidious fingers. He turned the thickest volume spine upwards. 'I thought so.'

'What is it?'

'Chambers's Dictionary.'

It had fallen open in his hand. I peered at it in the torchlight. 'So useful. Did you know what a cusk was? It says it's a torsk or a burbot. What d'you know? Crosswords, Charles.'

'As you say.' He shut the book on a puff of dust, and picked up another.

This was smaller than the dictionary, but had a more important look, with thick leather covers which, under their fine greying of dust, seemed to be elaborately tooled. He handled this gently, and when he blew the dust off I caught the gleam of gilding.

'What is it?'

'It's a copy of the Koran, and a rather gorgeous copy at that. Take a look.'

The paper was thick and felt expensive, and the Arabic script, beautiful in itself, was enhanced by the ornate designs which headed the Suras, or chapters. It was certainly not the kind of book I would have imagined anyone would throw out into a dusty room to be forgotten.

He laid it down without comment, and the light was sent straying further over the debris. It halted suddenly.

'See what I see?'

At first, among the grey anonymous rubbish, all I could distinguish was the shape of a battered violin, something that might have been a pair of roller skates, and a tangle of leather thongs and buckles and tassels which resolved itself eventually into a couple of bridles. Behind these and half hidden by them were two dusty objects that looked like ornaments. China dogs.

Even so, I stared at them for a good five seconds, I suppose, before I got there.

'Charles! Not your Gabriel Hounds?'

'Indeed and indeed.' He knelt down in the dust beside the tangle of leather. 'Hold the torch, will you?'

I watched him as he carefully lifted the bridles aside and the one of the china ornaments in his hands. I noticed with some wonder how gently, reverently almost, he handled the thing. He took a handkerchief out of his pocket, and began to wipe the dust away.

Slowly, under the gentle ministrations of the handkerchief, the thing emerged. It was a creature which might have been a dog or lion, about six inches high, made in vivid yellow porcelain with a glowing glaze. It was sitting on its haunches with one paw down, and the other poised delicately on a fretted ball. The head was turned over one shoulder, at gaze, ears back, wide mouth grinning as dogs grin. It had a thick, waving mane, and its plumed tail curled over its back. Its air was one of gay watchfulness, a kind of playful ferocity. Its mate on the floor, her bright coat fogged with dust, had a plume-tailed pup under her paw instead of a ball.

'Well, my God, who'd have thought it?' said Charles softly. 'What do you think of them?'

'Heavens, don't ask me, I'm not up in these things. Are they really meant to be dogs?'

'They're what are known as Dogs of Fo, or Buddhist

lions. Nobody seems sure exactly what kind of creatures they were.'

'Who was Fo?'

'The Buddha himself. These are the only creatures
in the Buddhist mythology that are allowed to kill,
and then only in the Lord Buddha's defence. They're
officially the guardians of his temple.' He turned the
glowing creature over in his hands. The wrinkled
pansy-face grinned like a Pekinese over the pretty
ball.

'Do you know,' I said, 'I've a feeling I do remember
them. But why do you suppose they've been shoved
out here? I mean, I'd have thought—'

'Yes,' said Charles. He set the dog down again on the
floor, straightened up abruptly, and took the torch out
of my hand. I got the impression he hadn't heard a
word I'd said. 'Shall we get on with the programme?'

Without waiting for an answer, and without another
glance at the contents of the room, he led the way
quickly back into the corridor.

Here was silence and darkness, and the still smell of
unused, dusty air. The trees of the faded, painted
landscape slid past, punctuated by the dark cave-
mouths of empty rooms. Then ahead of us the corridor
curved slightly to the left, and on the outside of the
curve the torch picked out another doorway, the same
arched shape as the rest, but very different. Here was
no empty cave, no sagging and rotten timber. The arch
was blocked with a door of oak, brand new and solid as
a ship, and it was not only shut fast, but locked with a
new brass padlock.

The light paused on this for a moment, then moved on to the next door. Here again a new lock winked.

I said under my breath: 'The real treasure chambers, huh?'

My cousin didn't answer. The light slowly raked up the door to the barred ventilator above it, and down again, to fix on what stood beside it. He walked over to look, and I followed him.

Between the two doors, stacked against the wall, were a dozen or so cans, the size of small petrol cans, bright yellow with some sort of design on them. As the torchlight caught them I saw on the nearest, in bold black lettering: FINEST COOKING OIL *Ideal for Frying. Mayonnaise, Salads.* And below this, something else. I stopped.

The light came back to me swiftly. 'What is it?'

'On the tins,' I said, blinking in the beam, which swept down from my face again to the pile by the door. 'I just noticed – I can't remember where I saw it before. Oh, yes, now I've got it! It's nothing, Charles, only that design on the cans in red, the running dog.'

'Yes? What about it?'

'Nothing, I suppose. It's not important. Just that I've seen it before.'

'Where?' I looked at him in surprise. He sounded interested, even sharp.

'Sunday afternoon, up at the village Hamid took me to. I told you, didn't I? The sunflower field with the little sign on the tree-trunk, the red dog that I thought looked like a saluki.'

'This is the same?'

'I think so.'

We stooped closer, and now under the drawing of the running dog I could see in smaller black lettering: *Hunting Dog Brand. Best quality, beware immitations.*

'Sal'q,' said my cousin, half to himself. The torchlight was full on the tin. He looked absorbed.

'What?'

'That's what "Hunting Dog" is, did you know? The word "saluki" is the Arabic *seluqi* or *slughi* and means "hound". I imagine the Nahr el-Sal'q is some sort of corruption meaning 'Hound River'. Local produce, in other words. This is the same as you saw in the field?'

'Exactly the same.' I straightened up. 'Local produce it will be – sunflower oil, I suppose, and what I saw was a marker for the field. I think I read somewhere that the peasants use markers like that for their crops – I suppose it's sense, when a lot of them can't read. Heavens, this must be about ten years' supply! What on earth do you suppose they use it all for?'

He lifted one of the cans and put it down again, 'Empty,' he said shortly, and turned away.

I looked at him curiously. 'Why so interested?'

'Not here,' he said, 'not now. Let's finish this, shall we? And we'd better stop talking.'

When we rounded the curve of the corridor, going warily, we saw some thirty yards ahead of us a stairway, a wide sweep leading up to a landing and another elaborate arch. The door was standing open, back to the wall, but in its place, a heavy curtain hung across the arch. And at one edge of the curtain a line of light showed. We stopped still, listening. Even our own breathing sounded loud to me in the dead air. But nothing moved; no sound came from beyond the curtain.

Carefully shielding the torch with his fingers, so that only a rosy crack of light showed to dance like a fire-fly towards the curtain, Charles mounted the stairs and inched his way forward across the landing to the doorway. He paused beside the curtain, with me at his elbow. The torch was out now, the only light the streak at the curtain's edge.

Still no sound. But now I could smell the curiously pungent scent of Great-Aunt Harriet's tobacco. This must be the Prince's Divan. She might be very near us. She must have been reading, and have fallen asleep over her book. I couldn't hear her breathing I thought but then the room was so vast, and if she had drawn the bedcurtains before she slept . . .

My cousin put out a stealthy hand and drew the edge of the curtain back a couple of inches. He laid an eye to the crack, and I stooped to look.

It was certainly the Prince's bedchamber. And this was actually the curtain at the back of Great-Aunt Harriet's bed.

There was very little light in the room; the streak at the curtain's edge had only seemed bright in comparison with the outer darkness where we stood. The lamp stood on the table, its flame turned low, the smallest slug of light. But knowing the room, I could see fairly clearly. It was exactly as last night; the red lacquer chair, the unwashed dishes on the table, the hypochondriac clutter on the dressing-chest, the dish on the floor with DOG now half-hidden with milk for the cat, and on the bed . . .

For one breathless moment I thought Great-Aunt Harriet was there too, within a yard of us, sitting where she had sat last night in her welter of shawls and silks; then I saw the room was empty. The dark corner at the bedhead held only the tumble of blankets, and the red of her discarded jacket and the fleecy pile of the shawl.

A moment later it hit me again, the cold wave of sickness and the shiver over the flesh, as the cat lifted its head and eyed us from the tumbled bed. Charles saw it at the same moment as I did, and as I backed sharply away he let the curtain fall and came with me. His arms went round me.

'Okay, okay, it's not coming.'

'Sure?'

'Of course. You're all right, love, relax.'

I was shivering, and the arms tightened. The top of my head came just up to his cheekbone. 'Give it a minute,' he whispered, 'then we'll go.'

He held me like that for a while, till the shivering quietened, and I felt the cold leave my body. It was very dark and still. I knew from the sound of his breathing that he had turned his head away, and was watching and listening. He turned back, and I felt him draw breath to speak, then with an abrupt but stealthy movement his cheek came down against my hair.

'Christy—'

'Yes?'

A tiny pause. The breath went out like a light sigh, stirring my hair. 'Nothing. All right now?'

'Yes.'

'Come along then.'

'You – you really didn't want to wait and see her? I don't think somehow—'

'No. Forget it, we'll go back.'

'I'm sorry, Charles.'

'So you should be.' His whisper mocked me gently. 'Brace up, love, it can't get you. Be a big brave girl. Charles'll fight the nasty cat for you.'

The terror receded. I laughed. 'Big brave Charles,' I said. 'What if we meet the dogs? I'm fine now, thank you.'

'Really? Then we'll call it a night, I think. Back to your harem, my girl.'

The painted door was still wedged open, and the air outside in the pavilion was wonderfully fresh and sweet. We crossed the bridge to the gap, and I jumped it after him. He didn't let me go straight away.

'Christy . . .' He spoke softly, quickly. 'There's something I've got to tell you.'

'I knew it. I knew you were holding something back. Well?'

'Not quite that. I don't *know* anything. I've been making a few wild guesses, let's say. And I know that there's one thing very wrong, and it makes me smell a hell of a big rat. But – and I want you to take this if you will – I'm not going to tell you here and now.'

'Why not?'

'For the simple reason that you've got to stay in this place until morning, and I haven't. No, listen Christy

. . . you've got to meet John Lethman and be civil and normal to him, and you never know, Great-Aunt Harriet may take it into her head to see you again, and—'

'"Civil and normal" to John Lethman? Then there *is* something wrong about John Lethman?'

'I told you I was only guessing. Most of it's only a guess. But you have got to stay here.'

'So the less I know the better?' I said derisively. 'Corny, Chas darling, corny! Blast you, I can *act* innocence, can't I? I'm doing it all the time. Don't be so maddening! If it comes to that, it's me that's in the middle of this, and not you! Come on, you've got to tell me! Is John Lethman Aunt Harriet's lover or something?'

'Heavens,' said Charles, 'if that were all . . .'

I argued, of course, but he wouldn't be moved. Eventually he let me go, and prepared to jump back across the gap. I said: 'Why do you have to go back that way? Why don't you just shin down now from the window with the rope?'

He shook his head. 'It's easier this way. Close the shutters now, will you, so there's nothing to catch the eye? Don't put the bar back yet, just in case. I'll go now. You get yourself to bed, I'll see you at the hotel in the morning.' He seemed to hesitate. 'You're not scared, are you?'

'Scared? Why on earth should I be scared?'

'Well, as long as you're not,' said Charles, and left me.

II

So free from danger, free from fear,
They crossed the court: right glad they were.
S. T. Coleridge: Christabel

I THOUGHT I wouldn't have slept well, but I went out
like a light for the five hours or so until my breakfast
came, and woke to a glorious morning, and the sunlit
peace of the Seraglio garden with the ripple of water
where a light breeze touched it, and the singing-birds.

All the same, I remembered that I came back to
consciousness not of the romantic peace of the place,
but of the incipience of something cloudy, the faintest
shadow of apprehension colouring the day ahead.
Even when I realised that this was probably only the
result of Charles's hints about John Lethman, whom I
would have to meet again this morning, and the rest of
the day would be shared with Charles himself, I still
found that the Seraglio Court, the whole palace locked
in its hot valley afflicted me with a sort of claustro-
phobia, and I got up quickly and swallowed my coffee,
restlessly eager now to get out of the place and back to
the hotel and the life and colour and vulgar bustle of
Beirut. And to Charles.

Hamid had been told to come for me at half-past nine, but it was barely half-past eight when I finished the coffee that Nasirulla had brought me, lingered for a few minutes for a last look at the garden with the sun on the pavilion's golden dome, then let myself – by the orthodox route – out of the Seraglio.

My first apprehension had been removed by Nasirulla's appearance with my breakfast. If he were here, the river must be passable this morning. I decided to go immediately, and walk up to the village to meet Hamid there. I had tried to indicate to Nasirulla by signs that I wanted to leave early, and though he had merely stared at me in his unsmiling way without a hint of understanding, he must have told John Lethman, for I met the latter coming to meet me in the second courtyard, where the anemones of the Adonis Gardens had already, in the one day's heat, withered and died.

I thought he looked the worse for wear this morning, and wondered if the same could be said of me.

'You're up early,' he said.

'I suppose I must have been worrying about the ford. I gather it's all right and I'll be able to get across?'

'Oh, yes. Did you sleep all right in the end after the alarums and excursions?'

'After the—? Oh the dogs. Yes, thanks. Did you shut the poor things up? I admit I was a bit scared at first, but they were rather pets, and it's just another romantic episode to think about later on. But they're not like that with everybody, are they?'

'By no means. You must have something special.' A smile that didn't reach his eyes. 'I wouldn't say they're ever exactly savage, but they make good guard dogs, simply because they make a hell of a row if they hear anything out of the ordinary, I did shut them up, and it may have been a mistake.'

I didn't want to ask him why, but he had paused as if he expected it, and it was certainly the natural question. At least the pause gave me time to get my face in order, I asked: 'Why?'

'I should have left them on patrol. We found the side gate open. Anyone could have got in during the night.'

'The side gate? Is there another gate, then?'

'There's one opening out on the plateau at the back. What with that, and letting the hounds into the Seraglio, Jassim seems to have had himself a ball yesterday.'

I said, as casually as I could: 'But would anyone break in? You don't mean you've found signs of something?'

'Oh, no. It's just that universal trust isn't a habit of mine, particularly since I came to live in this country. What time's your driver coming?'

'Nine,' I said, lying, 'but I thought I might as well take myself straight off, and walk over to meet him in the village. You've been terribly good to put up with me for so long. I know I said it all to you yesterday, but you can take it today that it's easily doubled.'

'It's been a pleasure. Well, I'll see you out.'

He didn't even try to sound, today, as if he meant it. Yesterday's calm had vanished, and he seemed harassed and edgy. He hurried me through the smaller court with quick, nervous strides, a hand going to his face in that gesture I had noticed the first day, as if the skin was tender. He was sweating a little, and his eyes looked inflamed. I noticed that he didn't look at me, but kept his face turned away, as if self-conscious or ashamed. I wondered if he were being hag-ridden by the need for a 'smoke', and looked away, embarrassed.

'Your Adonis Gardens are dying.'

'Yes, well, they're meant to.'

'Of course. She doesn't know I came back?'

'No.'

'I didn't expect you'd tell her, it's all right. I just wondered if she said anything more about my cousin.'

'Not a word.'

Short, sharp, and to the point. Well, he owed me nothing but my escape. And far from preventing that, he was as eager to get rid of me as I was to get out. He walked out of the main gate with me, and right to the edge of the plateau, and stood there to watch me start down the path. When I reached the ford I looked back, and saw him still there, watching as if to make sure I really went.

I turned my back on Dar Ibrahim for the second time, and trod carefully out over the stepping-stones.

These were clear now, and already dry, but the water that swirled round them was higher than the last time I had crossed, and still ran iron red, blood red for the dead Adonis. Twigs, leaves, scarlet flowers, had been rushed down the stream and strewed in debris on the banks. Two of the goats browsed desultorily among the jetsam, but I could see no sign of the boy. As I gained the far side of the stream and picked my way up the